TEMPTING TEACHER

CRYSTAL KASWELL

Copyright

This is a work of fiction. Similarities to real people, places, or events are entirely coincidental.

Tempting Teacher
First Edition. May 12th 2022.
Copyright © 2022 Crystal Kaswell.
Written by Crystal Kaswell.
Cover by Hang Le.

Also by Crystal Kaswell

Pierce Family

Broken Beast - Adam

Playboy Prince - Liam

Ruthless Rival - Simon

Tempting Teacher - Max

Dirty Rich

Dirty Deal - Blake

Dirty Boss - Nick

Dirty Husband - Shep

Dirty Desires - Ian

Dirty Wedding - Ty

Dirty Secret - Cam

Inked Hearts

Tempting - Brendon

Hooking Up - Walker

Pretend You're Mine - Ryan

Hating You, Loving You - Dean

Breaking the Rules - Hunter

Losing It - Wes

Accidental Husband - Griffin

The Baby Bargain - Chase

Inked Love

The Best Friend Bargain - Forest
The First Taste - Holden
The Roomie Rulebook - Oliver

Sinful Serenade

Sing Your Heart Out - Miles
Strum Your Heart Out - Drew
Rock Your Heart Out - Tom
Play Your Heart Out - Pete
Sinful Ever After – series sequel
Just a Taste - Miles's POV

Dangerous Noise

Dangerous Kiss - Ethan
Dangerous Crush – Kit
Dangerous Rock – Joel
Dangerous Fling – Mal
Dangerous Encore - series sequel

Standalones

Broken - Trent & Delilah

Come Undone Trilogy

Come Undone
Come Apart
Come To Me

Sign up for the Crystal Kaswell mailing list

Chapter One

OPAL

The hotel bar is the perfect place for an illicit tryst.
Adult.
Anonymous.
Upscale.

This isn't a college party. Not even a college party at my famously fraternity-free university.

It's close to a high school party, really, given my background. Prep school, rich kids, thirty-million-dollar apartments overlooking the park.

The setting is right. But the sounds are all different. Soft jazz and quiet conversation, not hip-hop and truth or dare.

Which is more accurate?

Truth. Are you here to meet a stranger for a one-night stand?

Dare. I dare you to find Max and kiss him.

I take a deep breath and push an exhale through my nose. I don't fit into this world, not completely, but I understand it. My brothers thrive here. They've taught me how to blend into the demure, tasteful space of the rich and powerful.

And, hey, I have a fake ID, and I lie about my age. Max will believe I'm twenty-one. Probably. Hopefully.

I run my fingers over my leather clutch as I scan the space. A couple in a corner booth. Two women in suits, talking business. A working girl at the bar.

And there, in the other corner, a man in a suit and a hot pink tie.

Max.

The sliver of silk pulls me toward him. It's all I know about him, physically anyway. He's in a hot pink tie. I'm in hot pink shoes.

We match in the best possible way.

I take steady steps toward him. Slowly, he comes into focus.

Broad shoulders, dark hair, dark eyes, light skin.

The hot pink tie against his stark white shirt.

He's…

Perfect.

Not at all as I imagined him and exactly as I imagined him.

Handsome and powerful and intense.

His eyes stop on mine. They study me carefully, taking in every detail.

The intensity should unnerve me, but it doesn't. I want all his attention. I want him staring like I'm his favorite painting.

That's the other thing we have in common.

Art. And a mutual desire for him to tie me to his bed.

I stare back into his eyes. Nod a hello. Let my lips curl into a smile.

He doesn't smile back. Instead, he holds up his hand and motions *come here*.

On anyone else, the gesture would annoy me.

On Max?

Fuck. I'm already in over my head and we haven't even said hello.

With every step, my heartbeat picks up. My temperature rises. By the time I arrive at his table, I'm on fire.

He stands. "Opal?"

"Did the shoes give it away?"

His eyes flit to my feet. "They suit you."

"Thank you." My stomach flutters. "The tie suits you." Really. He has the high contrast complexion to pull off the whole bright pink on white on black thing. He looks bold and sexy and masculine all at once. I love that he's wearing pink. I love that he's secure enough to sit in a fancy hotel in a hot pink tie. I love that he's teasing me.

I already like him.

We've agreed to one night, and I already like him.

Fuck.

"Max." He offers his hand.

"Opal."

"Your coat."

I let him take it. "Thank you."

His fingers brush the back of my neck. He traces a slow line across the wool, then he shifts the coat off my shoulders and folds it on the booth. "Sit. Here."

I nearly drop onto the leather bench.

He sits next to me, at the curve of the bench, so he's perpendicular, so he can touch me and look me in the eyes at once. "Comfortable?"

"Yes. Thanks."

"Do you drink?"

"A little."

"What do you like?"

What can I order to sound elegant and mature? Without trying too hard? I don't know wine. Or cocktails. Or anything besides expensive whiskey and cheap vodka. The two alcohol choices of the prep school crowd. The booze from Dad's study or whatever they can convince someone outside the liquor store to buy for twenty bucks.

"It's not a trick question."

Is it that obvious I'm nervous? "Spicy."

"Only spicy?"

"Sweet too, but mostly spicy."

"Fitting." He smiles.

My heart skips a beat. His smile is gorgeous. Perfect. Addicting.

Max hails the waitress. Orders two cocktails, something called tropical heat, and asks for privacy.

"Of course, Mr.—Max." The waitress spins on her heels and leaves.

"Do you come here often?" My cheeks flush. "Sorry, that's a cliché, isn't it?"

"Don't apologize for feeling nervous." He looks me in the eyes.

We're not supposed to share personal details. That's one of our rules. But we can handle a little small talk. "Do you like it here?"

"I do."

"What do you like about it?" I ask.

"The company."

My blush deepens.

"Have you been here?"

"I've been to this type of place. My brother attends a lot of fancy events in hotel ballrooms. I come with him sometimes."

"Do you like them?"

"I like dressing up and sipping craft cocktails. But hotels always look like hotels, no matter how hard they try to make them look nice. And there's something sad about them."

"The transparently corporate attempt at decor?" He motions to an abstract painting on the wall.

Shades of grey in the shape of a martini glass. It's completely competent and utterly uninteresting. "I hate it, too."

"What would you put here?" he asks.

"What would you?"

"To fit the mood?"

"If that's what you want to accomplish."

"We're in an expensive hotel," I say. "It should feel that way."

He nods in agreement.

"But it should be specific too. So travelers remember they're in New York."

"The best of the MoMa?"

"Maybe. I do like pop art. But I don't think it fits here. I'd do something simpler. Photography maybe. Black-and-white panoramas."

"The skyline?"

I nod. "Too obvious?"

"Obvious isn't bad."

"Maybe the MoMa then. Prints of the most famous paintings from New York museums."

"To assert your cultural superiority?"

"New York is the greatest city in the world."

"Have you been to that many?"

No, but I am a born and bred New Yorker. "Enough."

"Were you born here?"

"How did you know?"

"I can always tell."

"You're not a New Yorker?"

"No, but I've come to appreciate the charms of the city. And its citizens."

Fuck. I must be as pink as my shoes.

"You have the best art in the US."

"I know."

"Should I compliment the coffee now?"

"Who needs coffee when you have art?"

"What's your favorite painting?"

"In the city?"

He nods.

"Drowning Girl. Lichtenstein."

"The MoMA."

"I go almost every weekend."

"Alone?" he asks.

"Usually."

"You're self-reliant."

Because of the painting? Or because I go on my own. "I am."

His gaze shifts to the waitress.

She steps into our space with a smile and sets two drinks on the table. Something bright pink, in a martini glass with a chili sugar rim. "Enjoy."

"Thank you," Max says.

She leaves with another smile. Is it friendly or interested? No, it doesn't matter. She's doing her job. I'm here for one night with him, and he's being polite.

I may be nouveau riche (sort of), but I'm never an asshole to servers. Even when they're assholes to me.

"Try it." He pushes one glass to me. Picks up the other. "If it isn't to your liking, I'll order something else."

I bring the drink to my lips and take a sip. The kick of pepper, the sweet, fruity flavor of pineapple, and a depth from the cranberry and orange liqueur. "Perfect."

He swallows. Coughs. "Spicy."

"You think?"

"You don't?"

"A little."

"Are you one of those people?"

"Which people?"

"With an obscene tolerance for spice?"

"So I hear."

"Does that mean you enjoy pain?"

"I haven't tried it." Not really. "Not with someone I trust."

"Do you trust me enough?"

"Yes."

"Are you sure?"

"No."

He smiles. "I appreciate the honesty."

"You won't change your mind?"

"No. I want you to stay honest. I like your sincerity."

My cheeks flame. It's hot in here. It's way too hot in here. I take another sip, but the drink does nothing to cool my temperature or calm my nerves.

Still, it feels rich.

Rich and complex, with the perfect mix of heat and sweetness.

Like Max.

"It's brave," he says. "Admitting vulnerability. Admitting inexperience."

"Thank you."

"Okay."

"You remember the safe-word?"

"Cranberry."

"I'm not planning any scenes. Not for a first time. Unless that's what you're looking for."

"A scene?"

"A role-play scenario."

"Do you do them?"

"Sometimes. It depends on my mood. My partner."

"Do you want to do one with me?"

"No," he says. "I want to be who we are. Two strangers, meeting at a bar, for one night of adventure."

It sounds sexier on his lips.

Or maybe it's the reality. We're not trading texts about times and preferences. I'm not wondering if he's short or tall, thin or muscular, handsome or less handsome—

He's here, and he's just right. Even though he's not the tallest or the broadest or the most typically handsome.

I prefer the intensity of his features.

The perfect height—in my heels, I'm a little taller than he is.

The lean muscles.

He's just… right.

"Does that work for you?" he asks.

"Yes."

"Is there anything else you haven't mentioned? An injury or a medical condition?"

"I'm allergic to dairy."

He finishes his drink. "Is there anything I've missed? Anything you want me to know?"

One night. No last names. No details. All dirty promises. "Nothing comes to mind."

He stands and offers his hand. "Then I'm ready whenever you are."

Chapter Two

MAX

Opal shifts in her seat, straightening her back, projecting pride and strength.

Bravado or an awareness of her power?

I'm not sure.

She's gorgeous, sweet, eager.

And I'm already hard, watching her pretty red lips part.

She captured my attention with her first message—*I know this isn't why we're here, but I have to say I love the painting behind you.*

She stopped to discuss art.

My kind of woman.

But that's why I shouldn't be here—

I want more than one night. I already know that.

I want to take her home and teach her everything I know.

Right now, I don't have a home. I don't have a place for my life, much less hers. And she's beautiful and sweet and inexperienced.

She's sunshine, and I'm darkness, and I can't bottle her light.

Opal swallows a sip of melted ice, stands, offers her hand. "I'm ready."

She's tall—eye to eye with me in her heels—and she

radiates power. Not the conventional, masculine idea. A feminine one. The softness, vulnerability, ability to admit her desires.

She's gorgeous. Long, slick, straight dark hair, deep blue eyes, slim curves. She's young, maybe too young to drink at a bar, but I don't care.

I need tonight.

I need to be the person to introduce her to this.

I take her hand, gather her coat, lead her out of the lobby to the elevator bank. The finance bros standing in the space shoot me a *way to go, dude* look.

For a second, I think of Raul's crooked smile. He fit into this world. He knew how to work with these kinds of men.

When he told me our start-up would be *epic*, I laughed, but he was right. He made the two of us a fortune.

He was like Opal. Light and sunshine.

Or so I thought.

Given current events—

Fuck. I'm not here to dwell on past mistakes.

I'm here to get out of my fucking head. To push the clouds aside the only way I know how.

Opal is sunshine, and I won't be her storm cloud. That's all I need to know.

This is a fair deal—I introduce her to a world of play in exchange for one night soaking up her rays—then I say goodbye. That's the only way to protect her.

No ugly memories, no awful labels, no fear of the future.

Only a gorgeous brunette coming on my hands, face, cock.

What better way to celebrate?

Or commiserate?

Or honor?

Whatever the fuck it's supposed to be.

The shiny doors slide open.

The finance bros step inside. Shoot us a *you coming* look.

I press my palm into Opal's lower back. Lead her into the elevator.

She looks to the men in suits with recognition, but she doesn't say anything.

The car stops on the fourth floor. One of the finance bros winks on his way out the door. He trades a laugh with his friend, something about a woman they want to share.

The doors slide together at a painfully slow rate.

Opal lets out a heavy sigh.

"Someone you know?" I ask.

"Only the type," she says. "My brother is in finance."

"Are you close?"

"We are. I'm closer to my oldest brother."

"How many do you have?"

"Four." She hesitates. "Three."

She lost a brother. I want to know more, to know everything about her, but she's not here to discuss ugly things. And tonight isn't about my depraved desires.

It's about hers.

"What's he like?" I ask. "Your oldest brother?"

"Like you," she says.

"Kinky?"

"No." Her cheeks flush. "At least, I don't think so. God, is he? He's *always* busy with his girlfriend. Like a high school student with his first love. But I guess that's fitting, since they met in high school. Shit. I'm rambling, aren't I?"

She is and it's adorable. "Don't apologize."

"He's quiet and serious sometimes and funny sometimes. Protective."

Like me.

"And he commands the room the same way too. People fall in line. Something about him."

That isn't me, not the way she means, not as an executive. But here—

It is me here.

"Not that I'm thinking about my brother. Only that, well, they're all around your age, and they wear suits. But you don't look like them. So it's not weird. We all have blue eyes. And we're all white. Not that I'm curious about your ethnicity. Only it's not—"

"My mother is Japanese."

"I wasn't asking. It was more—"

"I know. You're nervous. It's normal."

Her cheeks flush.

My blood rushes south. She's adorable. And responsive.

I need to toy with her.

To find every spot that makes her purr.

But I need to be careful too. She's new to this. I need to be gentle with her. Not give in to my desire to fuck her hard and fast immediately.

I will fuck her hard and fast—

When I'm sure she's ready.

The elevator doors slide open. I press my palm into her lower back and lead her into the hallway, around the corner, all the way to the door.

I pull the key out of my pocket and press it into her palm. "After you."

She nods and slips the card into the electronic lock. *Click-click.* The light flashes green. The space opens.

She takes a deep breath and steps inside.

I hang her coat on a hook on the wall. "Do you want a drink?"

"No thank you." She flicks the light switch. Her big, blue eyes go wide as the room illuminates. She studies the space with interest. The narrow hallway, the leather armchair, the desk in the corner.

The skyline in the wide window.

Usually, New Yorkers annoy me, but there's something about

Opal's sincere love of the view. I want to watch her stare. I watch to see her in her space. Her room, her apartment, her city.

I give her a moment to move into the main room and take in the space. I wait until she's in front of the couch.

Then I start. "Are you ready?"

"Yes."

I make her wait. I silently count to ten. Fifteen. Twenty. Twenty-five.

Thirty.

Forty.

Fifty.

It's too quick—I should go to a hundred—but I'm impatient.

And she's already wound tight with anticipation.

This is it. The start. One night with the gorgeous brunette. One night of sunshine, then I release her.

I stare into her beautiful blue eyes, and I begin. "Take off your dress."

Chapter Three

OPAL

Take off your dress.

Max's voice echoes off the clean white walls and wide glass windows.

It flows into my ears. Sure. Steady. Enticing.

This is happening.

And I'm not just nervous. I'm terrified. But he likes that. He likes my honesty.

I take a deep breath and let out a steady exhale.

"Can you help?" I turn and motion to the zipper on the back of my dress. "Please."

He moves toward me slowly.

I pull my hair over my shoulder.

Max runs his fingers over the back line of my dress. Slowly, he pulls the zipper down my back and pushes the straps off my shoulders.

He peels the dress over my chest, stomach, ass.

The fabric falls at my feet.

I step out of it.

He brings one hand to my hip. Brings the other to my lower

back. "Beautiful." He traces a line up my spine with a perfect, impossibly light touch.

I need more.

I need exactly this.

All of this forever and ever.

My fingers curl into my palms. My eyelids press together. My thighs shake.

He traces the line all the way to the waistband of my underwear.

They felt mature and sexy when I slipped into them, but now, in this ornate space?

The cotton bikinis feel impossibly unsophisticated.

"Do you always match your underwear and your shoes?" he asks.

My lips curl into a smile. My cheeks flush. He's teasing me. He's not deeming my Natori French-cut bikinis too casual. He's trying to set me at ease. "If I can."

"I do."

"All black?"

"Yes." He curls one hand around my inner thigh. Draws it higher, higher, higher—

There.

His palm brushes my sex, pressing the soft fabric against my skin. It's quick, a second, but it still sets me on fire.

Fuck.

I need more.

I need everything.

He traces the lace trim over my ass. "Take these off."

I slide the panties off my hips. Kick them off my feet.

"Turn around."

I do.

He watches me carefully, studying me with his deep brown eyes. They're dark, intense, impossible to read, and impossibly intriguing.

He's more handsome than I imagined. Richer too. The room, the suit, the watch—they're all expensive.

After years as an official Pierce, I know how to spot wealth. It doesn't move me the way it did once, but I do notice. Max is loaded.

He didn't mention it. He didn't try to entice me with status symbols.

He asked what I wanted and offered to give it to me.

A perfect gentleman. In a twisted way.

He looks me up and down slowly, savoring every inch. "I could do this all night."

A whimper falls from my lips.

He smiles. Proud. Secure. Completely aware I'm putty in his hand. "I won't."

"Promise?"

"No." He looks me over again. "But I promise you'll leave satisfied."

My chest flushes.

"Come here."

I meet him in front of the armchair.

He sits. Cups my hips with his hands. Looks up at me like I'm a painting he's admiring. Then it's something darker, something dripping with desire.

He turns me around and pulls me backward into his lap.

My legs part reflexively.

My hips rock.

He's hard. I need more of the friction. Fewer of the layers.

My skin against his.

Max presses his lips to my neck.

Softly at first.

Then harder.

Harder.

The soft scrape of his teeth.

My fingers curl into my thighs.

The pressure is perfect. Not enough to hurt. Only enough to feel I'm his.

Only for tonight. But for tonight.

With the next brush of his teeth, I surrender to the sensation. I let my eyes fall closed. I let my lips part. I let a groan rise from my throat.

He slips his hand between my legs. Draws a line up my thigh.

Higher and higher—

Closer and closer—

There.

His thumb brushes my clit. Soft. A hint of pressure.

Then more.

More.

Exactly enough.

"Fuck." The word falls off my lips.

He hears. Keeps that perfect pressure. Tests different strokes.

A little faster.

A little slower.

Bigger.

Smaller.

There.

I let out a groan. Reach back for him reflexively.

He wraps his hand around my wrist. Hard. "Only if I say." His grip stays tight. "Exactly what I say."

I nod.

He places my hand outside his thigh on the couch cushion. Takes the other and does the same. "Keep them there. Or I stop."

No. Not that. Anything else but not that. "Yes."

He groans against my neck.

The vibrations make me buzz.

I want to please him. It's the only thing I want. It's the only thing in the world.

Everything else is fuzzy, far away, out of frame.

This is in sharp focus.

The rough wool of his jacket.

The soft brush of his lips.

The murmur of his breath.

Max brings his thumb back to my clit. He teases me with soft, slow strokes, again and again.

Then he speeds.

There. The pressure I need. The movement. The pace.

Again and again.

Closer and closer.

The tension inside me winds tighter and tighter.

Again and again, until it's almost too much to take.

Then I'm there, digging my hands into the cushion, groaning as I unfurl.

Everything goes white.

The perfect, pure light of bliss.

He works me through my orgasm. Then he pulls his hand back. Wraps his fingers around my wrists. "This way."

He wraps his arm around my waist and helps me to my feet.

His body stays pressed against mine.

His cock stays pressed against my ass.

He holds me there for a long moment, then he takes a half-step backward.

He presses his palm into my lower back and leads me through the living space, into the clean, minimal bedroom.

King bed. Clean white sheets. Oak dresser. Matching desk covered in notebooks.

Is he staying here? Or did he come early, to set up the room, prepare, feel at ease?

Visions form in my mind. Max, curled in the armchair, notebook in hand, thoughts focused on a project.

What does he do all day?

What does he draw when he's alone?

What does he want?

My thoughts scatter as he releases me. I pull them back. To the room. The gorgeous view of the Manhattan skyline. The clean white bed.

Max, at the dresser, pulling a condom from a drawer.

He slides the foil packet into his pocket. He does away with his jacket.

The tie.

The watch.

Slowly, he rolls his sleeves to his elbows.

Fuck, his forearms are sexy. How can forearms be this sexy?

How can I be so enamored with his bare forearms when I'm buck naked?

He meets me at the edge of the bed. "No circulation issues?"

"None."

"You're sure?"

"Yes."

He nods. "Makeshift materials are fun, especially for roleplay, but they're not safe. If you want something that *really* restricts you, you need bondage rope."

"And this?"

"It's only tight enough you'll feel it." He presses his lips to my shoulder. "Put your hands behind your back."

I do.

He presses my wrists together. Gathers the tie. Cinches a snug knot. "Feel this?"

I nod.

"Move your hands."

I wiggle my fingers.

"Not tight enough to truly restrict movement. Now this—" he pulls the knot tighter. So tight it cuts into my skin. "This isn't safe. If I leave this too long, I could cause permanent damage."

"How do you know?"

"Practice." He loosens the knot. "Two fingers is a good rule of thumb." He slips two fingers under the tie. "If I can't get two fingers under a binding, it's too tight. You won't be able to test yourself. You'll have to trust whoever you're with."

And he doesn't trust my future partners.

He's protective of me.

Which is strange. We agreed to one night, one time.

But then I like the way it feels too. I want Max protecting me. Even if it's only tonight.

"Get used to the feel." He tugs at the knot until the tie digs into my skin. "I hope you'll always have a partner who looks after you, but I can't count on that." *Unless I come back and tie you up again.*

It's there, in his voice, but neither of us mentions it.

"This feels okay?" He tugs again.

I dig my nails into my palms. "Yes."

"Good." He places his body behind mine again. Presses his lips to my neck again.

Soft.

Slow.

Tender even.

He slides his hand around my waist, holds my body against his as he kisses a line down my neck, over my shoulder.

Then back up.

The scrape of his teeth.

Harder.

Harder.

Hard enough I feel it.

Hard enough it hurts.

Then he moves me. Not to the bed.

To the wall.

He pins me against the cream wallpaper.

Slowly, at first.

Then fast.

Hard.

I turn my head, but still, my temple digs into the wall.

Fuck.

It hurts in a way that feels so fucking good.

My thoughts disappear as he tugs at my hair. "You're pliable."

I don't know what to say, so I nod.

"It's driving me out of my fucking mind." He brings his hand between my legs. Slips two fingers inside me. "You're perfect, Opal."

Fuck. That's intense.

He pushes his fingers deeper.

Deeper.

Adds a third.

My eyes flutter closed.

He drives his fingers into me again and again, spreading me wider, pushing deeper.

When he pulls back, I'm empty. Achy. Impossibly in need of satisfaction, only he can provide.

He rocks his hips against me, so I feel his hardness against my ass.

One tease, then his hands are on his slacks. The belt. The button. The zipper.

Max knots his hand in my hair. He holds me in place as he tears the foil wrapper, rolls the condom over his cock.

Then he brings one hand to my hip, and he pulls my body over his.

His cock strains against me.

The sharp tug of rubber.

The light hint of sensation.

Only enough to make every molecule of my body scream *more*.

Again.

Again.

All at once, he pushes into me.

Fuck.

My eyes close.

My fingers dig into my palms.

My toes curl into my heels.

He pulls back and does it again.

A little faster.

A little faster.

There.

A groan falls from my lips. I reach for something, but the tie catches my wrists. I need more. I need to do something to release the pressure building inside me.

My groan gets louder.

My nails dig harder.

His name falls off my lips.

Max wraps his other arm around my torso. He pulls my body into his, holding me close as he drives into me again and again.

Pushing me closer.

Closer.

So fucking close.

But so fucking far too.

Then he tugs at my hair and slips his hand between my legs.

Again, his thumb brushes my clit.

No teasing this time.

Only that perfect pressure.

He rubs me as he drives into me.

It's too much to take.

But, somehow, it's not enough either.

I'm greedy. I want more. I want every fucking inch of him.

My hips rock of their own accord.

With his next thrust, I come. The tension in my sex unwinds, sending pleasure all the way to my fingers and toes.

That perfect white light. Only brighter, purer, even more beautiful.

Then he's there, scraping his teeth against my neck as he pulses inside me.

He works through his orgasm, then he untangles our bodies, takes care of the condom, shifts into his slacks.

He returns to the bed, to me.

For a moment, he holds me close.

For a moment, we stay in that easy, seamless space, locked together. Then he releases me, unwraps my wrists, and rubs my sore skin with his palms.

He sits up and shifts into a different version of himself. Still caring and in control but softer.

"Have you eaten?" he asks.

"Yes."

"Do you want anything?"

"Anything at all?" I ask.

"Before round two."

"Can you…"

"Not yet. But I'd make you wait either way." His smile is easy, reassuring.

He feels safe.

He feels way too safe.

I should leave now, before I get attached, but when will I get this chance again? "How many times?"

"Enough."

Enough. Fuck.

He moves into the bathroom, runs the sink, emerges with two glasses of water. "Drink."

My fingers brush his as I take the glass. The same electricity passes between us. Stronger even.

He watches me finish the glass, refills it, watches me drink another. "I got you something."

"Oh?"

He reaches into the dresser and pulls out a white gift box held together with a fuchsia ribbon.

"Is it pink?"

He mimes zipping his lips.

My stomach flutters. "May I?"

Satisfaction slips into his voice. "Please."

I take the box, set it on the bed, unwrap it.

Sure enough, it is pink—a deep, sultry shade of magenta—and it's perfect. A silk chemise, equal parts elegant and punk rock princess.

"Thank you."

"Put it on."

I nod and pull it over my head.

"Go into the main room," he says. "And wait."

"For what?"

"For me to decide what to do with you."

Chapter Four

OPAL

For three minutes, I wait.

For three minutes, my body hums with need and desire.

For three minutes, every one of my thoughts tunes to Max.

Then a noise cuts through the space.

The buzz of a... cell phone. And that *I'm trying not to sound annoyed because it's unprofessional* tone of voice. I've heard it on my brother Simon a million times. It's never good.

Max ends the call and knocks on the door. "Opal." He shifts to a matter-of-fact tone. "I have to end this early."

No. I only get one night. This isn't enough. I need more.

"Something came up. A favor for a friend. I wish I could turn him down, but I owe him too much. I'm sorry."

"I understand." I look for something to cover myself. A robe or a t-shirt or a pillow even.

He knocks again.

At first, I don't register it. This is his hotel room. I'm following his commands.

But I'm not. Not anymore.

This is over. We're shifting into some other place. In this place, he asks for permission before entering the room.

I barely muster a "come in."

He opens the door, but he doesn't move into the room. "It's not you. I promise."

I force my lips into a smile. "I understand."

He doesn't buy my happiness. "I wish I could make it up to you, but…" He lets me fill in the blanks. We said one night, one time, and he's happy to stick with that. "Stay if you like."

"I don't know." I feel stupid in his hotel room without him. "I don't have anything to wear."

He motions *come here* again.

This time, I do.

He brings his hands to my shoulders and pulls me into a tight embrace. "I am sorry. I hate breaking promises." He runs his fingers through my hair. "If it's any consolation, I'll be hard as a diamond at this meeting."

"The entire meeting?"

"With a very important person who could make my life difficult."

That's hard to imagine. Max seems like he's the very important person. But I guess we all have someone.

My brother Simon is the CEO of the family company. He doesn't answer to anyone at work, but there are plenty of people capable of making his life miserable.

For Max, who knows? I guess I never will. I can imagine any story I want.

He's a spy on an assignment to seduce the president's daughter.

He's a lawyer, and his best client was just arrested for murder.

He's an artist who will draw pictures of me forever.

"All night probably." He releases me and he fixes his clothes. Sleeves, watch, jacket. Then the cell and wallet. "Here." He reaches for something in the dresser. Pulls out another clean white shirt. "If you decide to stay."

"I'll sleep naked."

He smiles, charmed by my willingness to make him regret leaving. "If you don't."

"Well… we can play who wears it better."

"Do you really think you can beat me?" His smile lights up his dark eyes.

My stomach flutters.

My heart thumps.

I cinch the middle button and strike a pose. "How do I look?"

"Dashing."

"But not perfect?"

"No." He reaches for his tie. "You need this." He drapes the pink around my neck and cinches a loose knot.

"Do you want it back?"

"Keep them. I have to go." He presses his lips to my neck. "Goodbye, Opal. It was a pleasure meeting you."

"You too."

He looks me over one more time, shakes his head *damn, the injustice of the world*, and he leaves.

I wait until the door slams shut then I do away with his shirt and tie.

I don't know what to do, so I shower away the day, I wrap myself in a fluffy towel, I slide into the soft silk sheets.

For a few minutes, I think of salvaging the rest of the night. Calling my friend Izzie and asking if she wants to go dancing or even come over here and watch *Gossip Girl*.

But I'm not ready to see anyone. I'm not ready to talk about this.

It's mine.

After another ten minutes of tossing and turning, I fall asleep.

I wake alone to a cold empty room and a note from Max, from last night.

Thank you for a satisfying evening. I'm sorry I had to end it early. I wish things were different.

The room is yours until check-out.
Help yourself to anything.
Take care,
Max

———

My ride home is quick. And cold. My heels aren't designed for January mornings. The dart from my rideshare (I refuse to use the service my brother hires—then he'll know where I go) to the apartment building is frigid.

The second I step inside, warm heat envelops me. It's too much, too hot. Not just because of my thick wool coat. Memories of Max threaten to send my temperature skyrocketing.

I push them aside. Perfect my story, the one I need to tell my brother.

Simon is my oldest brother and my legal guardian. At least, he was, until I turned eighteen. I grew up with my mom. I didn't know my father. I didn't believe her stories about him being a rich, powerful man, about wealth and power waiting for me.

But they were true. My father was the previous Mr. Pierce, an old money billionaire who didn't want anyone to know he knocked up the help. So he paid my mom to keep my heritage a secret. And, when she died, I found the paperwork to prove it.

The next day, I showed up here, at Simon's apartment (it once belonged to the previous Mr. Pierce). He didn't know he had a half-sister. He was as surprised as I was. But he welcomed me into his home, his life, his family.

He's caring, intelligent, more fun than he lets on, and incredibly over-protective.

Which is a massive problem at the moment.

If he knows I spent the night with an older man—I'm not sure how old Max is, only old enough Simon will object—

With a stranger—

Tied up in a stranger's hotel room—

He'll ground me for life. And, yes, technically, I'm an adult with a trust and the power to make my own choices. But this is his place, and he pays my tuition, and he—

Well, he's my favorite person in the world. He's everything I wanted in a father. And just like I imagined when I was a kid, I'm terrified of disappointing him.

I take a deep breath and practice my story.

I spent the night with Izzie. We didn't do anything special. The usual. She's still asleep but I have homework. The semester started last week, you know. And the school promised a replacement for Professor Barba by the end of the week. No doubt, he's going to assign two-hundred pages of reading to make up for the missed classes.

It's perfect. True enough—Professor Barba did die suddenly, and I am sad to lose him—and focused enough on acing schoolwork to distract Simon from the whole *did you fuck someone last night* thing.

After another deep breath, I climb the stairs and let myself into the apartment. The massive penthouse is quiet except for a familiar song. One of those mid-aughts pop numbers Simon and Vanessa play.

I get it. They attended high school together when this song was popular. Simon wants to hit his girlfriend's nostalgia buttons. That checks out.

But how can Vanessa and Simon, both the picture of refined elegance, swoon over *Collide*?

I guess it's kind of fun, in an over-the-top sappy way, like a CW show. It's not enjoyable if I take it seriously, but if I let go and embrace the ridiculous?

Thrill ride.

Unfortunately, Simon is only lost in the music for about five seconds. He notices me immediately.

"Morning." He looks up from his spot on the couch. "How was Izzie?" His voice stays even and utterly without suspicion.

Which is highly suspicious. This is probably a new game, to trick me. "You know Izzie."

"Wanted to stay in and watch *Riverdale*?"

"She's got a crush on Jughead."

His nose scrunches with distaste. "The kid with the dyed black hair?"

"He's cute."

"Because he's a bad boy?"

"Yes, Simon, that's how we teenage girls think. All men fall into three types: nerd, jock, and bad boy."

"Which type am I?" he asks.

"Suit."

"That isn't included?"

"It's a nerd subtype."

"Liam is a nerd subtype?"

"Liam is obviously a jock."

"Adam?"

"Adam could not be more of a nerd. Are you kidding?" No signs of Vanessa in the room. No coat on the rack or shoes by the door. She's not here. But, judging from the music and the satisfied look on Simon's face (gross), she was. Maybe that's why he's calm and trusting. Cause he got laid (also gross).

"Who's the suit in *Riverdale*?"

"The hot dad."

"And is this your type too?" he asks.

"No, I like all types."

He makes that same *ick* look.

"Would you prefer if I liked girls?"

"I worry about you."

"In a very sexist way," I say.

"Probably. But I'm trying."

Damn, he's not giving any push-back today. Is he setting up a trap or just… happy?

"Did you eat?" he asks.

"Not yet."

"Coffee?"

"You can make the coffee, but, Simon, please don't try to cook."

He smiles and falls into our usual banter. "I can toast bread."

"Can you?"

"Usually."

"The toaster caught on fire last time."

"And look at our replacement toaster." He motions toward the kitchen.

I follow him around the corner. Take in the hot pink toaster with a smile. Over the last three years, I've added *a lot* of pink to the place, but this is one of my favorites.

Simon and I fall into our usual routine.

He fixes dark roast with the French press, warms coconut milk, toasts bread, brings jam, utensils, and plates to the kitchen island.

I fry eggs in olive oil and pick a hot sauce.

Simon chuckles as I set the sambak olek next to my plate.

"Yes?" I open the yuzu marmalade and spread it over the slightly under-toasted bread.

"You always stare at the hot sauce for minutes then pick that one."

"It's always a rooster sauce day."

"And always this one over sriracha."

"Please, Simon, sriracha is for babies."

He smiles at the familiar comment. "What did you and Izzie do last night?"

I check the button on my coat. "We went dancing at an all-ages club. Then we watched *Riverdale*."

"That's a busy night."

"Only for someone your age."

He doesn't take the bait. "You don't have to make up a story."

I reach for my coffee. Will the sweet, creamy dark roast to kick my brain into *read Simon properly* gear. "Thanks for the coffee. It's perfect."

He looks to the dress again. My fingers. My neck. "I'm sure you wouldn't lie to me unless you felt it was necessary."

Do I have a hickey? I don't bruise that easily, but Max was… aggressive.

"If you do have a relationship with someone, a man or a woman, and you spend the night… You can tell me that. As long as you're being safe, I'll respect your decision."

Now, I'm suspicious. "Really? If I want to have a threesome with the guys in my art class, you'll respect that?"

"You've used that one before."

"The question stands." I take another sip.

"Yes, Opal, as long as you're using protection and you trust your partner. Or partners."

"Really? No matter what?"

"I trust your judgment," he says.

"No matter what?"

"Should I not?"

No. I just… expect more resistance.

"If you're ever in over your head, you can ask for help."

"With sex?"

"Anything. Including sex." He pauses. Studies me again. "The world isn't a fair place. Women often pay the consequences for men's indiscretions."

"What do you mean?"

"Do you really not know?"

Sort of. Mostly. But not exactly the way he means. Simon is in his thirties. He's surrounded by older people, with older ideas.

His concept of the "the world" is different than mine. More… dated.

But I did spend the first fifteen years of my life not knowing I had four brothers.

Not knowing I had a rich, famous (late) father.

My mother and I paid those consequences, but Mr. Pierce suffered his own. He didn't get to know me. He didn't get more time with my mother. He paid in his own way.

"You're an adult now. You'll pay for your decisions like an adult. The consequences won't always be fair. Look at Briar and Liam. She was his assistant. They started dating. Both adults, who made a choice. He was the one who took advantage of his position. But people don't whisper about him getting his job on his back."

It sounds so nice, in theory, my brother, the insightful feminist, well-educated by his activist girlfriend (and his own *I have a teenage half-sister* reading), but it's actually terrible.

It gives him all these extra insights into how fucked up the world is for women and how much more he needs to protect slash lecture me.

Okay, it's pretty cool in certain ways. And Simon has been a great "girlfriend" for a long time. He spends hours holding my bags when we go shopping. And he's a whiz with liquid eyeliner and crown braids.

He's… well, he's like a father looking out for his teenage daughter. He's not shy about figuring out any normal teenage girl things and participating when appropriate.

And, apparently, that now includes discussing my sex life.

Awesome.

So awesome.

"I appreciate the warning," I say.

"Do you?"

Sort of. "Yes."

He nods, accepting my response but not necessarily buying it.

Over an hour, and a second cup of coffee, Simon and I talk about the weather (freezing), our brothers (Liam is as difficult as ever, Adam is slightly less reclusive every day), school. He's concerned about my professor's death. The details he assumes someone suppressed—thirty-something men don't die suddenly—and the possible effect on my grades.

He's not heartless. He's just pragmatic. To a fault.

After I remind him we're not the injured parties—this really isn't our business—I excuse myself, spend a few hours drawing in my room. Images from last night. The bar, my heels in the air, Max's arm around my waist.

Then I take a run, shower, fix a frozen meal for lunch.

After a few episodes of TV, I check my email.

As promised, the school found a replacement for Professor Barba.

But my nine a.m. Monday morning class is the least of my concerns.

Because the replacement professor is someone I recognize.

Professor Barba's business partner.

Max Morrison.

The man who tied me to his bed last night.

Chapter Five

MAX

Raul and I met in college. We were perfect opposites. He was practical and charming, bright and funny. I was, am, artistic and guarded, dark and… well, I hope I'm witty, in my way.

He was sunshine, the way Opal was.

He was the light I needed. As a friend. Then, as a business partner. He knew how to sway me. He knew exactly what to say to convince me to join him.

I need your vision, Max. No one sees things the way you do. You bring the art. I'll bring the spreadsheets. One meeting a year, that's it. I promise.

I ended up in a meeting every few weeks, at first, but once we were running, he held to his promise. I stayed in California and advised. He moved to New York and lived, breathed the city and the company.

Every year, we met here for our yearly meeting and the party that came with it. A freezing December weekend in the city. A day of bullshit then, a night of drinks.

We toasted, the way we always did, to a year well done, to the secrets we were about to trade.

His divorce.

The distance between me and Cassie.

The CTO sleeping with his assistant.

He asked if I'd take over his class if something happened to him. It was a joke, after I said he was too drunk to walk home. At least, I thought it was a joke.

Now—

I can still see the relief in his eyes, the lightness in his shoulders, like he'd finally put his affairs in order.

Did he know then?

Did he have a plan?

Did I hand him a loaded gun?

All these years, I held on to my role as the broken one. I held it so tightly I ignored the signs. I ignored his need.

I failed him.

I can't fail him again.

All day, I sign papers, read guidelines, send emails.

I fill tiny boxes with ink scribbles until my mind and hands are numb.

After I finish, I take the subway to the sparse apartment the company provided, use the gym on the fourteenth floor, shower until the warm water turns cold.

I don't don my fleece pajamas. I don't turn up the heat. I climb into bed and try to sleep.

It's too cold. My mind races. The more I try to straighten my thoughts, the more my head spins.

My late best friend's warnings. His smile. The laugh we shared when we toasted to broken hearts.

His marriage.

My long-term relationship.

Failing in different ways, for different reasons, but failing all the same.

Then I think of her. Opal.

Even her memory is sunshine. It illuminates every pocket of darkness in my head.

For a few minutes, I try to resist temptation, but it's no use. The image of her wakes my body.

My heart pounds. My blood surges. My breath quickens.

I close my eyes. Give in to the images forming in my mind.

Opal, in jeans and a tight white tank top, sitting on my desk.

Tossing her top over her head.

Doing away with her soft pink bra.

Climbing into my lap, grinding against my cock as I suck on her perfect pink nipples.

I come quickly. Too quickly.

She's too sweet, too beautiful, too perfect.

I pull the covers to my chest and give in to my other physical needs, but the blanket isn't the kind of warmth I crave.

And the memory of her isn't enough.

But, at this point, what is?

EVERY MORNING IS THE SAME. FOR A SECOND, I SAVOR THE comfort of the sheets, the safety of the bed. For a second, I believe everything is normal.

Then I remember.

After I drag myself out of bed, I fall into my morning routine and head straight to class.

Students look at me with tired, uncertain eyes. They don't know me or trust me or believe the vague messages from the school about Raul's death.

Do any of them suspect the truth?

Did any of them see the signs?

The world is different than it was when I was in school. People know more about mental health. People talk about depression. People talk about suicide.

Not the way my mother does, clinging to ideals of honor—

Not the way my brothers do, rejecting her beliefs—

With respect for struggle and intense belief in saving lives.

They're more enlightened. But they're still young and myopic. Do they realize this can strike anyone, at any age, at any time? Or are they as foolish as I was?

I'm hopelessly out of place here. Too old, too out of touch, not experienced as a teacher.

But we are aligned in one way: we appreciate Raul.

"Good morning." I don't know where to start, so I start at the beginning. "I'm Professor Morrison. Professor Barba passed away a few weeks ago. I'm his official replacement, but I won't truly replace him. No one could."

The room stays silent.

"I'm sorry you've lost the professor. He was a great man, a great friend, and I'm sure, a great teacher. I will do my best to fill his shoes, but I'm sure you'd all prefer your first semester with him." I set the stack of papers on the desk of the student in the front-left corner. "The syllabus. Everything you need is on here. If you have any questions, see me after class. Please, pass these out."

The student nods *sure thing*. "Professor Morrison?"

"Yes?"

"I'm sorry for your loss."

My heart almost breaks again. My calm facade too. Kindness is too much to take these days. Especially from a stranger who was in my late best friend's class. "Thank you." I barely find my footing. "Let's have a moment, for Raul. Professor Barba. Then we can move on." I give him a full minute, an eternity in a room full of strangers, but not nearly long enough.

Then I begin.

Class moves quickly. I barely cover the necessary material.

"The reading assignment is in your syllabus and online," I say. "Any question, come by office hours."

Students pack their bags and file out of the doors in a chaotic fashion.

One by one, they move into the busy hallway, leaving the slow students and the ones who want to ask questions.

I answer one by one. Until a familiar voice greets me. "Professor Morrison."

And I see her.

The girl who spent the night in my bed.

Opal.

She's just as beautiful in jeans and a loose pink sweater. More even.

She waits for the last student to leave the room, then she trains her deep blue eyes on me. "I think we need to talk."

Chapter Six

MAX

There are many things I'm capable of doing.

Working sixteen hours straight, running an eight-minute mile, making a woman come.

Resisting dirty thoughts of Opal?

Not so much.

But they're my thoughts. Any awkwardness I feel around Opal is mine. She trusted me last weekend. I won't betray that.

"Is this why you left early?" She presses her lips together. "I'm sorry. It's none of my business."

"We're both adults."

"I lost my brother two years ago. I lost my mom two years before that. I know how hard this is. I'm sorry you lost your friend."

Kindness from Opal is far too much. I nearly melt on the spot. "Thank you."

"I don't want to make that harder but I... I really liked this class," she says.

"It's not a problem."

Incredulity fills her blue eyes. "It's not?"

"I didn't accept the position until yesterday."

"And you didn't know my last name. So how could you know?"

It's true, but it's not fair. I knew she was young. I knew it was within the realm of possibility. "It was one night. That's all. I can pretend it didn't happen."

"You can?"

"If you can."

"Sure… I, uh, well… I can't promise I won't think about it, but I'll do my best to keep it out of class."

She thinks about me.

It shouldn't move me, but it does.

"That isn't a problem," I say. "As far as I'm concerned, you're another student, one I met today."

"Okay." She plays with her backpack straps. In her normal college girl clothes, she looks impossibly young, small, in need of protection.

She isn't small—she's only a few inches shorter than I am in flat shoes—but she still radiates vulnerability.

She's still sunshine.

I still want to capture all her light.

I vowed to protect her on Saturday. I stand by that vow.

"If you aren't comfortable, I understand," I say. "I can help you find another class. Transfer."

"No. I'm… I'll get comfortable."

"Great."

"There is one other thing."

Come back to my place. I want to make you come. Immediately.

"I was working with Professor Barba on a personal project," she says. "I don't expect you to take over, but if you could help me find assistance with someone else…"

"I'm happy to help."

"It's personal," she says.

"Would you prefer someone else?"

"No."

"I won't be offended, Opal. I promise."

"I don't know your artistic abilities yet."

"Do you want to test me?"

"No. Your lecture was good. And your... thoughts on hotel lobby art."

"Is the project pop-art inspired?"

"It's still taking shape."

I want to see it. Every sketch, every page, every image. I still want her, all of her. Before it was a bad idea. Now, it's completely out of the question.

"We were meeting in his office, but—"

"Wherever you're comfortable." I don't even believe myself. "The library."

She sticks out her tongue. "I hate libraries. They're too quiet. Especially the one here, with the weird floor and the glass panels."

Both the floor and the panels are there to make it harder for students to attempt suicide. For years, the school was notorious for its suicide rate. The rate wasn't significantly higher than the average university, but because the school was large, and the deaths fit the narrative of New York City as an unforgiving place, the stories made headlines.

Does she know my best friend died by suicide?

Does it hurt her too, losing this mentor she trusted?

I swallow hard. "My office hours—"

"Are on the syllabus, yeah. I have class all afternoon."

"Email me. We'll arrange a time."

"Are you sure?"

"Are you?"

She nods and forces a smile. "It was nice to meet you here, Professor Morrison."

"You too, Opal—"

"Opal Pierce." She bites her lip. "Yes, my brothers run Pierce Industries. I'm sure you're familiar, with your work at Paytron."

She's being modest. Pierce Industries isn't quite as famous as Google or Apple, but they're a household name.

"It's really not a big deal," she says.

"I understand." Technically, I co-founded Paytron, but it was all Raul.

"I looked you up when I got the email about class. I looked up all my professors."

My head tries to latch on to the logic—I'm not special—but my body refuses. My heartbeat picks up. My blood rushes south. "Anything interesting?"

"There's no art under your name."

"That's right."

"Do you have a secret pen name?"

"If I told you, it wouldn't be a very good secret."

"Fair." She smiles, catches herself flirting, forces her expression to something neutral. "I hope we can work well together. I really do want to learn." She must notice the double meaning, because she blushes. "I, uh, I'll see you soon. Wednesday, I guess. Have a good day, Professor Morrison."

"You too, Ms. Pierce."

She smiles, charmed by me using her last name, then she turns and steps out of the door.

For a few minutes, I stand, dumbstruck, unable to think of anything except her brightness. Then students for the next class file into the room and I push my other thoughts away.

I channel my late friend, introduce a new set of young adults to his work, return to his office for my mandatory office hours. Every week, after the two classes I teach, Monday and Wednesday.

Most working professionals teach evening classes. Students in the arts have a particularly difficult schedule—most of their courses aren't offered until five p.m.—but Raul asked for mornings, so he could skip mandatory meetings at work.

He even volunteered extra office hours.

At the time, I thought he was being his usual difficult self, objecting to the attempts at authority from our new CFO and COO.

Now, I wonder if he was running away. Testing a different path to the end of his life as the head of Paytron Saint.

Why didn't he tell me?

No, he did. In a million little ways. But I found an explanation for all of them. Stress. Burn out. Difficulties in his marriage.

It's so easy to see the signs now.

Was I oblivious? Or was he that good at hiding?

For two hours, I cycle between thinking of my late friend, answering student questions (mostly requests for extensions), and drawing whatever comes to mind.

When my hours officially end, I have a list of students with approved extra time for assignments, four pages of drawings of the city at night, and eight sketches of a pretty brunette in my bed and… elsewhere.

There aren't defining features, but it's obvious.

That's Opal.

All day, I try to adjust my focus. I eat lunch, I draw, I help Raul's replacement transition.

The only thing that clears my head is my workout. For an hour and a half, I swim. I swim until I can't take another stroke. I shower and dress and fix dinner and think of Opal.

She's there, in my emails, politely suggesting times and a place to meet. She can come to the Paytron building if that works for me. It's close to her brother's office, and she meets him there on Tuesdays. A routine of theirs.

She's ready to pretend this never happened.

I'm not.

But I'll get there.

Chapter Seven

OPAL

All night, I check my cell for emails from Max.

Then all day Tuesday.

During class. During my workout at the school gym. During my ride to my brother's office. (Somehow, I avoid the temptation during dinner).

On my way to Izzie's place.

Every time she excuses herself to grab a snack or use the bathroom.

I'm not sure what I want more—a request for round two or a promise we're strictly professional.

Both.

Either.

Is it that easy for him to forget our night?

Is he interested in mentoring me as a teacher or more?

I check again.

This time, Izzie catches me.

"Opal Pierce, that is the third time you've stared at your phone longingly," she says. "Are you waiting for a dick pic?"

"Gross."

"Are you waiting for a pussy pic?"

"Also gross."

"Then why are you staring at your cell like you want to lick it?"

"I am not," I say.

"You are so." She plops next to me on the couch. Peers over my shoulder, trying to view my screen. Then my sketchbook.

I try to press the pages together, but she's too fast. She sees the outline of a drawing. One of Max.

It's hard, drawing from memory. I can't capture the contours of his face. I can't put every detail to paper. Only the feeling of his presence. Power, pride, generosity, sadness. The drops of pain I saw in his hotel room and the river I saw after class.

If my best friend died—

Izzie and I aren't as close as we were in high school, but I'd still feel lost without her.

She was the only person at our elite private school who really saw me. The scholarship students wrote me off as a Park Avenue Princess. The rich kids wrote me off as a bastard daughter.

But Izzie… Izzie gets me. Her parents are rich too, old money snobs too, but she spent summers with her rebellious aunt and adopted her aunt's fondness for pissing off her mom.

She doesn't dye her hair blue or rock short skirts *just* because her mom hates it, but she would dye her hair green and wear torn jeans if her mom hated that more. (Though she'd kill me for saying that).

"Oh my god, who is this hottie?" She taps the sketchbook. "Is this the guy?"

"What guy?"

"The guy you met over the weekend. Who else?"

"There were so many guys," I say. "You'll have to be more specific."

"Yeah right, Opes. You're as sweet as your backpack."

"It's punk rock."

"It's bright pink."

"Yes. Punk rock femininity."

"You're the stylish one." She concedes my point. "And I'm the one who knows you're bluffing. Tell me."

"Tell you what?"

"About the guy. The weekend. What happened?"

"I told you. It was a date. That's it."

"A date at a hotel bar."

She knows the details. Well, the ones about us meeting online, texting, agreeing to a one-night thing. Not the ones about the type of activities were planned to enjoy.

"You also told me you really liked him," she says. "Even though you agreed it would be a one-night thing."

"I did."

"So… what was it like, meeting him in person?"

"Surreal."

She brushes a bright blue strand behind her ear and motions for me to continue. "Come on, Opes. You know my sex life is on hold until May."

"Didn't Jamie leave last week?"

"So you understand it's been days."

"How are you still insatiable?" They're high school sweethearts. They've been together a long, long time.

"I hadn't seen him since Thanksgiving,"

"So three weeks."

"But three months before that. Imagine if you and Max had been texting for three months."

"You mean, sexting and having phone sex three times a week?"

"You don't know, Opes. The phone sex starts three times a week. Then two. Then one. Then you're both saying you're kinda tired, and you're not sure if you're up for it, and you're wondering if that's because he met someone at the frat party his roomie 'dragged him to' and if he secretly wants to find a pretty sorority girl. Maybe a bottle blonde who spray tans. And then you're mad at yourself for judging another woman for her hair choices, and in a totally hypocritical way, because you bleach your hair too." Disappointment drops into her voice.

Fuck, I'm ignoring her. I'm a terrible friend. "Do you want to talk about it?" I ask.

"No. Maybe. I think we're good. You should have seen me at the airport. You would have thought he was going to war, not to California."

"California is basically war."

"Right? You know what the weather is today on campus?"

I shake my head.

"High of sixty and sunny."

"You mean he prefers warmth to wind tunnels?"

"Crazy, right?"

"Very." I press my sketchbook closed and sit up straight. "Was it hard, saying goodbye?"

"Miserable. I held it together until he went through security, then I was crying. Ugly crying."

"I'm sorry."

"Everyone warned me about long-term relationships."

"They don't know you," I say. "You're tough. And Jamie is too."

"Yeah, but sometimes I wonder if they're right."

"Yeah?"

"Maybe it is an anchor in a certain way." Her brown eyes turn down. "I hate myself for thinking that."

"Why? It's true. I… think it about us sometimes?"

"Bitch."

"Sorry."

"No, I get it. I see you and I see a private school uniform. And, well… I start to think about Jamie."

"He's your boyfriend."

"My first love," she says. "That implies a second, doesn't it?"

"Only if you want a second."

"I've said no to so many things because I wanted to call him. Because I missed him. Because I needed him."

I rest my head on her shoulder. "Do you regret it?"

"No. And I would hate to prove my mom right too. She told me to end things, so I could have fun in college. That I shouldn't get too serious with anyone until I'm twenty-five."

"Twenty-five?"

"That's when your brain is mostly finished developing. Kinda. It's more complicated than that. I think it's that she regrets marrying my dad so young, you know?"

"Do I know about distant fathers?"

"Yeah, right. But, ugh, I'm so tired of hearing myself whine about missing Jamie."

"You're not whining."

"Maybe not now, but in my head, and in my journal? If someone read it, they'd think I'm some kind of crazy stalker. It's *I miss Jamie* again and again. Like one of those old-school detention assignments to write on a chalkboard a hundred times."

"I'm sorry it's so hard."

She pulls an invisible zipper over her lip. "No more complaints about my love life. I want to hear yours instead. The sexy bits especially."

"Won't that make you think of—"

She mimes the zipper again.

"Won't that increase the problem of your horniness?"

She laughs and play swats me. "I can live with that."

Okay, well, I can deliver here. "We talked a little at the bar. He made sure I was comfortable. Then we went up to the room and he told me to take off my dress…"

She stares at me, hanging on every word. "He was bossy?"

"Clear in his preferences."

"What was he wearing?"

"A suit."

"Was he here on business?"

"We didn't trade that info."

"You're really never going to see him again?" she asks.

"We only agreed to one night."

"No. Wait. Back to the sex. You took off your dress, then…"

"He…" I hold up my hand.

She smiles. "He was good?"

"Very. And then we went to the bedroom and went against the wall."

"Hot. Kinky."

I fight a blush.

"We, uh, not that I'd ever talk about my long-distance relationship, but I floated something like that with Jamie."

"Oh?"

"I mean, say I did, say I was with someone—"

"Just talk about him."

"He shut it down," she says. "He's not game."

"Is that okay?"

"I don't know. I think… fuck, my mom might be right. I want the space to experiment. To try things. But what do I do?" she asks. "Either way, I miss him. And better to suffer and prove my mom wrong, right?"

"Does that make her suffer?"

"I think so."

"Makes sense to me."

She smiles. "How was your goodbye?"

"Abrupt. He had an emergency."

"You didn't get the entire night?"

I nod.

"So he owes you more."

"Maybe." It's a compelling argument.

"Is that why you're checking your phone all the time? Waiting for more from him?"

"Sorta."

"Check again."

"Are you going to look over my shoulder?"

"Do you want the truth?"

Okay. It's not a secret. And it's not like Izzie would share this with anyone. She's loyal.

I unlock my cell. Pull up my email.

And it's there. An email from Max.

From: Professor Max Morrison
Subject: Meeting times
I'm ready to start Friday.

"You fucked your professor?" Izzie puts it together immediately. When I start to reply, she shuts me down. "Don't lie. You can decline to answer, but don't lie. It's obvious."

"I didn't know he was my teacher."

"Your brother is going to kill him. That would be hot. Simon is so—"

"My brother. Gross."

"And hot."

I clear my throat. "It happened before he was my professor. You saw the story about Professor Barba. They were business partners. And friends."

"When did that happen?"

"About two weeks ago."

"So you were his distraction, huh?"

I guess so.

"Do you think you were a good distraction?"

"Don't objectify me."

"But you thought it too, right?"

I did. "I hope so."

"And now, what…"

"Now, I'm going to go to his office Friday and pick up the work I was doing with Professor Barba."

"Alone?"

"Alone."

"And you're not going to fuck him again?"

"That's the plan."

"Do you really believe that?"

"What's the alternative?"

"He left early, right?"

He did.

"So he owes you the rest of the night. After your study session... ask for another kind of study session."

"You watch too much porn."

"I don't watch any porn."

"Then you have too many dirty fantasies," I say.

"Oh really? I'm the one with dirty fantasies? You're not sitting here, doodling your professor naked?"

Ahem.

"Show me the sketches then. If he isn't naked in them?"

"No comment."

"You're considering it."

"No."

Maybe.

"Really, Opes, lie to yourself if you want, but don't lie to me."

―――

For the next two days, Izzie and Simon duke it out in my brain.

She stands there, blue tendrils falling over her heavily lined eyes, badass and ready to proclaim her sexual desires to anyone who listens, yelling *go after what you want.*

And he stands there, in his crisp charcoal suit, shaking his head *you want to be treated like an adult? This is what it means to be an adult. You acknowledge consequences and make hard decisions.*

And then the pain in Max's eyes chimes in. Reminds me he's suffering and in need of understanding. And also in need of distraction. And possibly thinking about me naked too.

Between class, workouts, homework, studying, and dinner,

they fight for supremacy. When I can, I push them aside and pour my thoughts into my art project, the one I was pursuing with Raul.

It's personal. I didn't feel comfortable sharing with him at first, but it was the only way to get his help. And Raul hadn't seen me naked or heard me come.

This is it.

This is what wins: My need to grow as an artist, express myself, find space.

I can't do that if I'm sleeping with Max. Or trying to sleep with Max.

I need to do as he's asked, and pretend it was someone else, somewhere else.

But… given the actual content of these drawings—

This is difficult.

Friday afternoon, I spend all my time polishing my project. I talk myself into ignoring the desire in my core or the flutter in my stomach.

I sip coffee; I eat an egg and avocado sandwich for dinner; I take the subway to Max's building, move through security, take the elevator to his floor.

The office in the corner, with the light on, that's his.

And it's the only occupied office.

Max and I are spending Friday night together.

Alone.

With no one to stop us from crossing the line.

Chapter Eight

OPAL

"Good evening." Max stands, moves around his desk, offers his hand. "Did you find the place easily?"

I shake with a steady grip. It's strange, touching him in this all-business manner. Somehow, it screams both *I need that hand between my legs* and *I'm absolutely not thinking about your hand between my legs*. "Yes. It's close to my brother's office." I'm here to work. I need to stay professional, but I need to stand on my own too. I'm not Opal Pierce, sister of the Pierce brothers. I'm Opal, the budding artist with the talent and tenacity to ask for help *and* deserve it. "I know the city well."

"I imagine." He motions to the plush armchairs in front of his desk. "Would you like to sit or stand? There's an easel in the conference room."

"Here? Really?"

"It's normally used for pie charts." He shakes his head. "The trouble with mixing art and business, business wins."

"It could be worse."

He raises a brow.

"It could be a spreadsheet."

He laughs. "Small victories."

"Exactly."

"Good attitude."

"I try." Like this, tonight. Max is now off-limits, which is tragic. He isn't going to sleep with me again. Also tragic. But he's here to teach me. He's volunteering his time and expertise. I'm going to focus on the win. Not on my desire to mount him.

In theory.

He looks so good tonight, in a sleek black suit and bright blue tie, his dark eyes intense and focused.

Fuck.

"Opal?" he asks. "Do you want to sit?"

I'd like to sit on your face. "Coffee?"

"Huh?"

"Do you have any coffee?"

"At this time?"

"At every time."

"In the kitchen. I'll fix it," he says. "How do you take it? We have almond milk and oat milk."

My stomach flutters. He remembers my allergy.

Get a grip. It's not a sign of love. He's conscientious, that's all.

"I'm particular," I say.

His lips curl into a half-smile. "I respect that." He offers his hand. "Shall we?"

"Thanks." My fingers brush his.

He pulls me to my feet and leads me down the hall, around the corner, to the small, clean kitchen. It's a lot like the space at Simon's office. A long counter with two sinks, a microwave, a drip coffee maker, another Keurig, an electric kettle, and said French press.

Besides the appliances, soap, and paper towels, the counter is clear. The snacks and coffee must be in the cabinet. Or the stainless-steel fridge at the end of the counter.

Max pulls a bag of beans from a high shelf, a blend from an expensive roaster.

"Are you a coffee lover?" I ask.

"Raul was," he says. "He was a sensualist."

"He seemed that way."

He nods and stays busy grinding beans, filling the electric kettle, setting the water to boil.

"Whenever I told him he had an artistic spirit, he said I should see his partner," I say. "I imagine that was you?"

"He liked to cultivate a reputation as a mercenary businessman, but he was a romantic at heart."

The kettle steams. Max waits for the temperature to fall to two hundred, then he fills the French press, sets the timer.

I find the almond milk in the fridge. It's a good brand, my go-to at a friend's house or a coffee shop (no one has coconut milk straight from the can).

"He wasn't ruthless," Max says, "but he had capabilities I don't, capabilities I'd never have."

"He read spreadsheets?" I ask.

A laugh spills from his lips. "He'd like that joke."

"Is it hard talking about him?"

"Yes, but it's good to remember." He looks to me. "What did the school say?"

"About his death?"

He nods.

"Nothing, really. The usual balance of 'he was impossible to replace, but here's this new teacher replacing him.'"

"Cynical."

"Maybe."

"Honest too," he nods. "He was… He was a lot of things I'm not."

"You're a good teacher."

"It's been a week."

"And you've done well. And you're here, volunteering help." And he did a fantastic job teaching me last weekend. But I can't say that. "I'm sorry you lost your friend."

"Thank you."

"My brother died in a car accident… almost two years ago now. It was sudden and tragic and I kept wishing I had more time with him. More time to get to know him, to soak up his joie de vivre. He was a lot like Raul. He had that same romantic spirit."

"I'm sorry."

"No, I… I'm not trying to take the space. That's what happened when my brother died. I had to be strong for my brothers. And I was glad to be there for them, but I wanted someone to be strong for me."

"How old were you?"

"Sixteen."

"When did your mother die?"

"Two years before."

"That's a lot of loss for someone so young."

"I know." My cheeks flame. Fuck. I'm doing this all wrong. "I'm not trying to—I just want to say I get it. I know it's hard. If you want to talk about it, I'm here. And if you need to stop because something makes you think of Raul, I get it. You don't have to explain."

"Thank you."

I want to say more. I want to do more. I want to throw my arms around him and hold him forever. He's holding it together, but I can see the cracks in his facade. And I know that feeling. It's hard.

But maybe this is what he needs. Maybe Izzie was right.

Our night was a distraction.

This, too, is a distraction.

But that's okay. It's romantic even. I'm the break in his day, the relief from his pain.

"I, uh, I promise the project isn't depressing," I say.

"Raul didn't leave any notes."

"I asked him to keep it a secret." But only because I was shy about the content. "Until it was done."

"Of course." Max half-smiles. "He loves the intrigue. I'm surprised he didn't mention you."

"Why would he?"

Max looks at me carefully, studying me, turning over some thought in his head.

About me? Or his friend? Or something else?

Maybe his desire to pin me over the counter and push my jeans to my ankles.

Beep.

The timer pulls me from my dirty thoughts.

Max turns to the French press, finishes fixing the coffee, pours the java into two clean white mugs.

I warm the almond milk in the microwave, add it to the coffee, stir in a spoonful of honey. "Do you want any?" I hold up the carton.

"Black."

"Really?"

"You don't like black coffee?"

"It's trying kind of hard, don't you think? The brooding artist who only drinks black coffee? What next? A beret and a box of Marlboros?"

"Is that the artist's cigarette?"

"No idea."

"Me either."

"Cigars and scotch then?"

"Where does the black coffee fit into this stereotype?"

"I'm still working on it."

He smiles. "Are you suggesting I drink it this way to fit some kind of role?"

"No. It's to stay in shape."

"It is?"

I nod. "You act as if it's a preference, because you're tough, but really, you want abs."

"How do you know I don't have them?"

"You do," I say. "And you want to keep them. It's your artistic vanity, wanting to be as divine as David."

"David, huh?"

The very famous, very naked statue, yes, and his well… relatively small dick. David, that is. Not Max. I didn't get to see Max up close, but I—

And now that's the only thought in my head.

Max naked and hard and ready for me.

My blush deepens.

"I can't believe you figured me out." He reaches for the almond milk and adds a little to his glass. "I don't drink milk."

"Lactose intolerance?"

He nods. "Not severe but enough I can't tolerate more than a macchiato."

"There's almond milk at every coffee shop."

"At every hip coffee shop in New York, maybe."

"Not where you're from?"

He smiles. "There too."

"Where are you from?"

"California."

"No."

"I'm afraid so," he says.

"The bay? Or the sunny part?"

"You realize the state is over seven hundred miles long."

"No," I say. "That means nothing to me."

"There's more than the bay and the sunny part."

"Which part?" I ask.

"The Pacific Northwest starts in Northern California," he says.

"So there are trees?"

"Lots of them."

"Are you from that part?" I ask.

"No. The sunny part. Orange County."

"Do you miss the trees?"

"The palm trees."

That doesn't fit the image I have of him. But I guess everyone loves home in their own way. "You're not one of those people who says they don't like the city because there aren't enough trees, are you?"

"I'm not."

"But you don't like it?"

"I like things about it."

"How did you end up here?"

"I didn't. I came for the funeral. Stayed for this."

And he's committed to the class for the rest of the semester. That's almost four months. "To teach Raul's class?"

"And help with the transition at the office."

"Did you come straight from Orange County?" *How long will you be here? When do you leave? How much time do I get with you?*

"Newport Beach."

"Like *Arrested Development*."

"They don't really film in Orange County."

"I haven't seen it," I say. "I like dramas."

"The *OC*?" he asks.

"Is it good?"

"It's not my kind of show."

"But *Arrested Development* is?"

"I don't watch a lot of TV."

"You're missing out. I watch *Gossip Girl*, even though it's about people like me."

"Beautiful prep school students?"

My cheeks flush. "Something like that."

"I guess you're the bigger person."

"Do you prefer Orange County?" I ask.

"Some things."

"Which?"

"The Mexican food."

Not the answer I expect, but understandable. We don't have a lot of Mexican restaurants.

"The sunshine."

Less understandable. Max doesn't seem like the type who loves bright days. He's brooding. But maybe that's why he loves the sun. Maybe he needs the light. "I love the winter here. The snow, the decorations, the atmosphere."

"The way the skyscrapers make wind tunnels?"

"Well…"

"Try spending the winter in California."

"Gross."

He raises a brow.

"My best friend… her boyfriend is attending college in Southern California. She's worried the sunshine will win him over."

"It happens."

"But how can a little sunshine be better than this—" I motion to the window. The office is dark, which means our view of the skyline is perfect. The soft indigo of the New York night sky, the grey and blue steel of tall buildings, the pockets and yellow and white light. "The city is alive."

"How did you get here tonight?"

"The subway."

"You stepped off a subway at eight in the Financial District and you're telling me the city is alive?"

"Yes, look—" I move closer to the window and watch the activity below. There isn't as much as there is at, say, ten a.m. on a Monday, but there are people walking home, heading to bars, ordering takeout coffee or gyros, eating standing on the sidewalk. "There's movement everywhere."

"You're one of those New Yorkers?"

"I am."

"Raul loved you, didn't he?"

"He didn't make grand declarations."

"Did he talk about his life?" he asks. "His marriage?"

"I'm not that young."

He raises a brow.

"I know what it means when a man talks about trouble with his wife."

"Not always."

"Usually."

"Did he?"

"No. Why?"

"He was getting a divorce. But I'm sure it started before that." Max shakes his head. "I didn't mean to imply you were a part of it."

But he thinks it. That's what's going unsaid.

What the hell is he going to say when he sees my drawings? Fuck.

I take a long sip of my coffee. "Should we get to work?"

"I'm sorry, Opal. Truly."

"Because you still think I'm a home-wrecker?"

"Because you're young and you're his student and even if he did have feelings for you, even if you propositioned him, he's the one who needs to act responsibly."

Right. But then we're not talking about Raul anymore. We're talking about him. "He didn't," I say. "He was a gentleman. And that was important with my project."

"How is that?"

"The series… it's self-portraits."

He nods.

"Some are clothed. But others…"

He puts it together.

Some are clothed.

The others are naked.

Chapter Nine

MAX

F uck me.
　　I take steady breaths.
　　I focus on every note of my coffee.
Caramel. Hazelnut. Clove.

The taste of Opal's lips.

No, her lips are sweet from the honey. Is she always that syrupy sweet? Or only when she comes to my office to show off nude self-portraits?

What the fuck is wrong with me?

I'm a grown man. I'm capable of resisting a beautiful woman. Even if making her come is the only way to push the ugly thoughts in my head aside.

That's my problem, not hers.

I top off our coffees and lead her to the office.

She unzips her hot pink backpack, retrieving a sketchbook and a large folder.

"I'm still working out the final form of these," she says. "I've been trying different styles. Oil, acrylic, pastels, digital painting even. I guess that's part of the project. Experimenting." She hugs her sketchbook to her chest. "I only brought two of the originals.

The smaller ones. Did you want to start with those? Or with the sketches?"

"What's your vision for the project?" I keep my voice even, as if she's any young artist. As if I'm not desperate to see her naked again.

I'm an artist.

I've sat through a hundred figure drawing sessions. I've seen thousands of depictions of naked women. Erotic depictions even.

That's all this is.

It's not another glimpse of sunshine.

It's not the only light to brighten my darkness.

It's certainly not an invitation to fuck Opal.

"I didn't really start pursuing art until recently. The summer," she says. "My brother insisted I take a class, so I wouldn't have time to get in trouble. Not that I ever got in trouble." She shakes her head *he's ridiculous*. "I thought an art class would annoy him. Especially one with figure drawing. I mean, me seeing naked men, the horror, right?"

Usually, I'd agree with her. There's nothing inherently sexual about the human form. And there's certainly no reason to keep a young person from seeing other humans relax in the buff.

But the thought of Opal's eyes on another man—

Fuck, I'm already out of my mind.

What the hell is wrong with me?

"I thought it would be fun for me too," she continues. "Art was my favorite class in high school, and I loved to doodle in the margins of my notebooks, but I saw it as a problem, not a pursuit."

"Teachers wanted you to pay attention?"

She nods. "I struggled, especially during lectures. Somehow, drawing hearts or flowers helped me focus. I wasn't actively listening, but I still absorbed some of the information."

I haven't been in school for a long time. Teachers don't criticize my inability to pay attention, but others do. "I've gotten dirty looks in meetings."

"Were you doodling hearts and flowers?"

"Naked women, usually."

"Really?"

"Sometimes."

"Me too." She smiles. "I guess I see the teachers' points. I listened while I scribbled flowers. But when I started to really craft a drawing, to follow my thoughts through my pen… that became my focus."

"What did you draw?"

"Women in different places, poses, outfits. Usually they represented me somehow, but not always literally. It was like I was trying on different identities. Or trying to examine my mood from outside, deciding which shape or color best captured what I was feeling."

"That's normal."

"Is it?" Her cheeks flush. "My family isn't very artistic."

"They're all in business?"

She nods. "They don't even collect art. Well, my brother Adam does now, but only because his girlfriend is an artist. A photographer. And, well, her work is hot. She's always trying to find the line between erotic art and porn and, uh, straddle it."

"Is that how she describes it?"

"No, she's very high-minded."

"You don't respect that?"

"She's talented. And she's good at finding the line. It's just… kinda weird, knowing that's my brother's girlfriend. Knowing… her male model is probably my brother."

"Are the pictures explicit?"

"Have I seen his dick?" Her cheeks flush. "No. But somehow… what I have seen is just as erotic."

Fuck, I need a new topic. "He only collects her art?"

"Or art she likes. My other brothers… they wouldn't know

good art if it slapped them in the face. Well, Bash did, but… not Simon and Liam. You should have seen Simon's place when I moved in. Beige. All beige."

"Maybe his life was beige."

"And I finally brought color to it?"

"You doubt that?"

"It's one thing for you to say it." She smiles softly. "If I say it, I sound like a raging egomaniac."

"You think it?"

She shrugs, caught. "It's true."

"Lean into that."

"Lean into being an egomaniac?"

"Yes."

"How rich are you?"

"What's that matter?" I ask.

"The more money and power you have, the more people tell you yes, no matter what."

"They're afraid you won't take no well?"

She nods. "And you get so used to that, you don't take it well."

"It happens."

"I've seen it."

"With your brothers?" I ask.

"Sometimes. They're not as bad as most, but they're not as reasonable as they believe they are."

"Brothers never are."

"You have one?" she asks.

"Two."

"Older or younger?"

"One of each," I say.

"Really? You seem like an oldest brother?" Her eyes flit to mine. "Are they still in California?"

"One is. One is in London."

"How'd he end up in London?"

"Work."

"What's he do?"

"Finance." I pick up a sketchbook of my own, sit next to her, place it carefully over my pelvis. I can handle this conversation. But when she starts showing off her pictures? "Tell me more about your project."

"Where was I?"

"The art class you took to annoy your brother."

"Right. My family is old money, but I'm not. I'm… in a unique position." She doesn't mention the reality of her father denying her parentage. She knows I know.

"You grew up with your mother?"

"I did."

"What was her relationship to art?"

"She loved art, but she didn't have a lot of taste. We'd go straight from free Fridays at the MoMA to a night of CW shows. The soaps where everyone has sex with everyone else."

"I'm familiar with the concept."

"Have you ever watched any?"

"I've dated women who did."

"Really?"

I raise a brow.

"You seem… like you wouldn't be interested in women with low brow tastes."

"I don't date based on taste in TV."

"Reasonable."

It's other tastes. Not that I've indulged often. My ex-girlfriend didn't enjoy this kind of thing. We compromised. I believed the compromise was enough.

But it wasn't. I asked too much of her. She asked too much of me.

We were on the rocks for a long time, strangers, living separate lives in the same three-bedroom condo.

Then Raul—

When I packed for New York, I told her this was the end. I had no plans to return.

Cassie protested, claimed she wanted to be there for me, but she seemed relieved when I said no. She's like me, too much like me. We're both bound by duty. Neither of us wanted to end the relationship.

That would be giving up.

And we don't give up.

Now—

Now, I'm here, imagining Opal tied to my bed.

"Have you had many?" she asks, somehow reading my mind. "Many girlfriends?"

"Some." This isn't a safe subject. "Did you watch anything else with your mom?"

"Everything. We'd read the same books too."

"You read?"

"Do I not look like someone who reads?"

My eyes flit to her hot pink backpack. Her stylish cashmere sweater. "You don't, but that isn't what I mean."

"No, you didn't invite me here to call me a stupid home-wrecker?"

Does she really think that? "I didn't mean—"

"I know. I'm kidding."

Maybe she's trying to ease the tension, but she is upset by the implication. "Really, Opal. You didn't do anything wrong."

"I know."

"I don't know you well enough to know how intellectual you are," I say.

"Then what did you mean?"

"You're a visual person?"

"I am."

"Visual people often prefer the medium of film."

"Do they?" She traces the edges of her sketchbook. "I don't

know if that's true. I love to read. It's easy for me to see the scenes happening."

"You have a great imagination?"

She nods. "I don't need to see something created for me, on screen. But then plenty of unimaginative people read. So… maybe there isn't a correlation. I don't know. I love music, but I don't know much about it. I don't have great taste."

"What do you like?"

"No. What do you like? If there's anything embarrassing, then I'll tell you one of mine."

"We're here to work on your art."

"Then you should make me feel comfortable, like I can trust you with personal things."

True. If she were anyone else, I'd be trying to build a relationship. I wouldn't withhold because I didn't trust myself.

"What if I say I only listen to jazz?" I ask.

"It would fit with your black coffee image," she says. "And I wouldn't tell you anything."

"Indie rock?"

"How much work did it take to get you in a suit instead of a beanie and designer jeans?"

My lips curl into a smile. "You want embarrassing?"

"Ideally."

"And honest?"

"No, I want a lie." She shoots me a *get real* look.

"Taylor Swift."

"No," she says.

"Yes."

"How?" She sits up straight.

"I started, ironically, to mock my girlfriend."

"The recent one?"

No. Cassie hated anything popular. She was like me there too—all darkness and frustration. It was too much. Fire and fire. "It's your turn."

"No." She shakes her head. "We need to stay on this longer. Are you a full-blown Swiftie?"

"I'm a fan."

"Have you been to a show?"

"I took my niece."

"But you wanted to be there?"

"I wanted to experience the event with her."

"Uh-huh." She smiles wide. "Favorite song?"

"*Blank Space*."

"Me too. It's just… everything. She writes great lyrics."

"She does."

"You really believe that?"

"I do."

"Do you like other pop singers?"

"You first," I say.

"Okay. Taylor Swift. Back to you."

"Vanessa Carlton."

"You do!"

"And Tori Amos."

"Fiona Apple?"

"I love Fiona Apple."

"Are you being serious right now?" she asks.

"I am."

She leans closer. "Favorite song?"

"It's obvious."

"*Criminal*?"

I nod.

"You know she wrote that to prove she could write a pop song."

"I know."

"You swear you're not fucking with me?"

"Cross my heart and hope to die."

She stares, studying me, absorbing this new information. "What is it about the artists?"

"They share their secrets."

"And most people don't?"

"We rarely see into someone else's head. Even when we know someone well, we don't always know how they feel. We don't know their deepest, darkest desires, their fears, their burdens." Or you ignore their signs. Ignore every single fucking clue. "Is that your project?"

"Does it give you every one of my secrets?"

I swallow hard.

"Is that what you want? Do you want every one of my secrets?"

Chapter Ten

MAX

Do I want every one of her secrets?

I want every thought in her gorgeous head.

I want to see her stripped bare in every single way.

Fuck, I thought it was bad wanting to see her naked—

But this craving is deeper, purer, infinitely more painful.

"I want what's best for your project." It's bullshit, but it's true. I'm here to guide her, to honor my last promise to my friend, whatever that takes.

"I know." She forces a smile. "I'm teasing."

She is, but she means it too.

"People are always mocking Taylor Swift for singing about heartbreak. I don't have that kind of heartbreak. No ex-boyfriends of note." She studies my expression, trying to see how the news lands.

Is it obvious I'm relieved?

Is it obvious I want to bend her over the desk and fuck her senseless?

"Is she your role model?" I ask. "For the project?"

"I don't know… I didn't think about it." She looks to her work, shifts her focus to the pieces themselves. "It is confessional.

And there is an obvious influence from other artists. I guess I should show you."

"Please." I motion for her to *go on*. Tell my cock to cool it.

She takes a deep breath and peels the cover back. She flips through pages of graphite sketches and stops on a simple self-portrait. "Some are more metaphorical. Some are more literal. I have an entire series like this. I was thinking, maybe this is what I want to say."

The sketch is rough. A young woman in an elegant gown, sitting on a chair.

She turns the page, and the drawing takes shape.

The woman, on the balcony of a high tower, sitting on the edge of the railing, staring into the distance.

The woman in the ball gown, surrounded by a blur of figures of men in suits.

A fancy party.

A room alone.

Then she's undressing.

The picture isn't erotic, but my blood still rushes south.

I force a breath through my teeth. Force my thoughts to straighten.

This is a figure. An artist. Any figure. Any artist.

I focus on the lines, the composition, the mood. It takes every ounce of my concentration, but I manage to push my thoughts to craft and only craft.

Even as I turn the page and watch the figure step out of her dress.

Stretch out in her bed.

There are dozens of poses, some simple, some erotic,

For hours, I look over Opal's work, I advise, I sketch with her, I ignore the scent of her skin.

Eventually, we finish. I walk her to the subway. Shake her hand goodbye.

I go home. I fuck myself. I barely survive the week.

Rinse.
Repeat.

The next week is the same. Class Monday and Wednesday morning. Meetings at work. Laps at the pool in the building. Pages and pages of drawings in my sketchbook.

Every night, I try not to think of Opal.

Every night, I fail.

Friday, we meet, work on her project.

I smell her shampoo.

I guide her.

I soak up every bit of her warmth.

Then, we do it again the next week.

The next.

Valentine's Day passes without a text from Cassie.

The winter weather fades to spring showers.

I spend the week off school locked in my apartment.

And then, the next week, I meet Opal again. I'm tired and worn. I'm avoiding too much.

Thoughts of Raul.

Thoughts of her.

My intense desire to hold her.

I make it through our session. Barely.

She finally finds it, the style for her project.

And it's perfect.

She stands over my desk, staring at a row of paintings.

Three self-portraits. Each a different style. Dada. Impressionist. Cubist.

All naked.

"Maybe this is it." She studies the contour of her breast.

Or maybe that's me.

"The different styles, together." She looks to me. "What do you think?"

I need to be inside you. "What does it say?"

"Something about self-discovery."

"Does it feel right?"

She nods.

"Then it's right."

She smiles and throws her arms around me. "Thank you, Professor Morrison."

Fuck, she's close. Warm. Soft. "You did the work."

She releases me. "I… we should celebrate. Right?"

"We should get home. It's late."

"Celebrate in a boring way… we can go to the Met."

"It's closed."

"Tomorrow."

"Are you done?"

"No."

"Then you'll be here again next Friday."

She nods.

"And I'll see you in class. Until then"—I motion to the door—"I'll walk you out."

"And meet me at the Met tomorrow?"

"I'm busy." Busy fucking myself, trying to picture anyone else. "Maybe next weekend."

She beams.

My heart thuds against my chest. I want to capture that smile. I want to watch it forever. "Maybe."

"I'm going to celebrate this weekend. You can stay home if you want."

"I will."

She makes a show of pouting. "It's fun for you, not being fun, isn't it?"

"Very."

"I figured." She stretches her arms over her head, pulling her sweater up her torso, revealing a flash of her undershirt. "Okay. Subway. I'm exhausted."

"Call a car."

"That's what my brother would want."

"Is it what you want too?"

"Yes, but if I do it, he'll win."

"He wins by you doing what you want?"

"You have an older brother. How can you not get it?"

"I get it. But I've also learned I win when I do what I want." This, too, is bullshit. I'm not doing what I want. I'm doing everything *but* what I want. But it's good advice.

Opal shakes her head *ridiculous* but she takes the advice. She pulls out her cell and taps the screen a few times. "What are you doing tonight?"

"Going to bed."

"Tomorrow."

"Working."

"You really don't have fun?"

"I have my own kind of fun."

"Oh." Her cheeks flush. "Right. Of course."

It's not what I mean. I'm not having fun with other partners. But it's better if she thinks that.

"None of my business." She hugs her sketchbook. "I guess that's just a normal weekend for you. Our, uh, experience."

No. "Yes."

The light fades from her expression.

I'm storm clouds, blocking her brightness. Even trying to protect her, I'm stealing her sunshine.

Fuck.

The pain in her eyes guts me, but this is what she needs, a little hurt now to save a lot of hurt later.

"I enjoyed the time. I needed it. But that's all it was, Opal. One night," I say.

"You've been with someone else?"

No. "Have you?"

"Why do you care? If it didn't matter?"

"I don't want to see you with someone who will hurt you."

"The two-finger rule?"

"Anything."

"Because you want to protect me… even though the night meant nothing?"

It's obvious bullshit. There's no way to explain it. Or justify it.

"So you wouldn't care if I'd fucked Garret?"

"From your class?"

"I don't know another Garret."

"Is he your type?"

"What do you care?"

"Are you being safe?"

"It's none of your business." She presses her lips together. "Whatever. You're right. It was one night. It didn't matter."

"We're both adults. We've moved on." It's a lie. Or I'm desperate to believe it's a lie. "Shall we?" I motion to the door.

"No."

"I insist."

She bites her lip, annoyed by me ignoring her cues. "Fine." She sets her sketchbook on the desk and picks up her coat.

I take it reflexively. Slip it over her shoulders.

My fingers brush her neck.

She shudders and leans into the touch.

Shit.

I pull my hand away. Immediately, I miss her warmth. Not just the heat of her skin but the brightness that's uniquely her. It's fading with every second.

This is what I need to do, for her, for both of us.

I repeat the mantra again and again as I don my coat, carry her backpack, lead her to the elevator.

Sometimes, you have to be cruel to be kind.
You have to be cruel to be kind.

You have to be cruel to be kind.

It hurts, but it's better in the long run for everyone.

But no matter how hard I try to convince myself this is best for everyone, I don't believe it.

It's best for Opal. That's obvious. But it's not best for me.

I need her warmth, her joy, her sweetness.

I need her naked in my bed, coming on my face.

She wraps her fingers around the metal railing.

I take a deep breath and push an exhale through my nose.

You have to be cruel to be kind.

The elevator arrives at the lobby with a ding. The metal doors slide open. I block them with one arm, motion *after you* with the other.

She forces a smile, nods, steps into the lobby.

I reach for her reflexively, but I catch myself before I place my hand on her lower back.

I want to touch her, but it's my problem, not hers.

All this bullshit is my problem, not hers.

And if it hurts me worse, well—

I pay the consequences for following my dick into danger.

She walks through the lobby with fast steps. Opal bristles as she moves outside, but she doesn't mention the cold.

For a few minutes, we wait together in silence. Then her car arrives, I open the door for her, help her inside.

"I'll see you Monday," she says. "Have a nice weekend."

"You too."

"I will, thanks." She hugs her backpack. "I have a date tomorrow."

"Good luck."

"Thanks." She forces a smile. "I do want to thank you for your other education. Since I'll be putting some of my knowledge to use."

My fingers curl into fists. "Be safe."

"I will. Thanks. We're going dancing first." She names a club in Hell's Kitchen. "Have a good night." She turns to the driver and offers instructions.

The car pulls away from the street. I stand there, watching her leave, trying to convince myself she's telling the truth.

Trying to convince myself I don't care who she fucks or if she fucks a different man every night.

Trying to convince myself to think of something else.

I don't.

―――

For hours, I turn over Opal's words. Until I finally give in to the images in my head.

Her body stretches over my bed, her blue eyes wracked with pleasure, her long legs wrapped around my waist.

For a moment, I'm satisfied. Then I want more.

I want everything.

Again, I toss and turn.

All day, I try to ignore the thoughts of her date. I swim, I fix breakfast, I work.

At sunset, I give up on resisting thoughts of her. I give up on convincing myself her date is a lie.

It probably is.

But just in case it's not—

I check the hours on the club.

Open at eight.

At seven forty-five, I step into a cab.

I tell myself I'll keep my distance, watch from afar, respect her privacy.

But I don't believe it.

Chapter Eleven

OPAL

"What the hell am I doing?" I press my knees together. "I don't even have a fake date."

"Am I invisible?" Izzie taps her blazer.

"Izzie."

"What? I'm hot."

"True."

"You're hot. Why can't we be on a date?"

"You have a boyfriend."

"He doesn't know that."

"I don't like you that way."

"That either." She raises a brow and smooths her skirt. She's in a re-purposed prep school uniform, and she looks hot. Like one of those fetishized action girls in a Quentin Tarantino movie. "How do you want to try it?"

"What?"

She holds up one finger. Then two. Then her fist.

"That isn't possible."

"It is."

"You've actually tried?"

"With Alice." Izzie's ex, the one who stomped her heart junior year. Over the summer, she fell, hard, for Jamie.

"Which way?"

"Both."

"No."

"Yes. Too much for you?"

"Too much."

"I know. A strap-on."

My cheeks flush. Izzie is interested in anyone, regardless of gender expression, but she knows I'm strictly interested in dick. And I know she's strictly interested in Jamie.

Or is that changing?

"Are you and Jamie okay?" I ask.

"Let's not."

"Are you still… together?"

"Please, Opal. Not tonight."

"Okay." I check the subway car again. It's not crowded, but it's not empty either. There's an older woman across from us. She's too busy playing a game on her phone to notice. "If you watch the volume."

She laughs. "And you want Professor Hottie to believe you're on a date."

"I told him a guy."

"Should we call Liam?"

"My brother."

"Half-brother."

"Because that's less disturbing."

"It is. And you know he'd agree," she says.

"He'll agree to anything. It's a personality defect."

"True."

"Gross. So gross."

"One of his friends? One of your friends. Oh… Alex."

"I broke his heart."

"You did," she says. "Cold Opal Pierce dumping the quarterback."

"He wasn't the quarterback. We didn't even have a football team. Where do you get this stuff?"

"*Riverdale*."

"That didn't happen on *Riverdale*."

"The spirit is there."

It is. And despite our lack of a football team, Alex fit the popular high school guy stereotype to a T. "Do you think he'd agree?"

"Probably," she says. "But he's at Yale. Oh, what about the junior who had a crush?"

"Is he even eighteen?"

"Oh… you need them legal now?"

"Oh my god."

"You're going to make all his dreams come true… do you think it will last twenty seconds? Or thirty?"

"No. The club. How will he get in if he's seventeen?"

"The same way we will. Fake IDs."

"How do you know he has one?"

"I helped him find it," she says. "Is the horny virgin thing not doing it for you?"

"It's not."

"I guess you're stuck with me."

"No." I shake my head. "This is crazy. Max isn't going to show up—"

"So we'll have fun dancing together."

"What if he does show up?"

"Then he wants you so badly he stalked your date."

That's true.

"And he's as crazy as you are."

Also true.

"And he'll be so relieved by your lack of a man on your arms he'll take you right there."

"In front of everyone?"

"Yeah, in front of everyone."

"What if he thinks I'm a liar?" I ask.

"You are a liar. You lied."

"Not helping!"

"Why don't you find someone?" She pulls out her cell and opens her swipe-to-fuck dating App. "Ask him to meet you there?"

"Isn't that your profile?"

"And?"

"And they'll be there for you."

"They're guys. They don't care."

"Only guys?"

"We'll only swipe on guys."

"Why do you have a dating profile? You have a—"

"You promised you'd stop."

I did.

"And you're in no position to judge my sex life. You dared your professor to stalk you to a sex club."

"It's not a sex club."

"Then why is the top review on Google 'best sex club ever.'"

"It's not."

"It kind of is."

Kind of.

"We can find you a date at the club."

I'm out with my friend, dancing until I forget my crush, that's all.

"You're right," I say. "He won't show. We'll have a few hours of fun and go home."

"And watch *Pretty Little Liars*."

"And I'll make chocolate-chip pancakes in the morning."

"Are you sure you're not trying to seduce me?" she asks.

"Don't even."

"Don't, what? Flirt? I'm an excellent flirt."

The train pulls into the station. Our stop. Already.

Izzie stands and offers her hand. It's a sweet gesture, the kind of thing a boyfriend does, the kind of thing Max does. I guess she's stepping into her role.

"Not necessary," I say, but I let her help me up and over the gap between the train and the concrete anyway.

"In those shoes, it is." She nods to my pink heels. "Aren't you cold?"

"The price of fashion."

"The price of Professor Hottie imagining you in nothing but your heels."

Ahem.

"You think straight men are the only people with those thoughts?"

"Are you picturing me naked?"

"You're not my type."

"You're a terrible date," I say.

She laughs. "Let's reset."

"Okay."

"Say your line."

"Is that necessary?"

She nods *yes, go*.

"Are you picturing me naked?"

"Not yet, baby. I respect you too much." She blows me a kiss.

I stick out my tongue. "It's not funny."

"It is, actually." She leads me up the stairs, into the cold night air. "I'm usually the crazy one."

I pull my coat tighter. March weather is unpredictable. Some days are warm, some cold, some clear, some pounding rain. Thankfully, there's no rain tonight, but the temperature is more suited to riding boots and wool socks. My toes are already freezing.

"Are those worth it?" She motions to my shoes again.

"They will be, if he's here."

"You think he's here?"

"No. But… maybe there is someone else, someone who will help me forget him."

She laughs.

"Hey!"

"Did you really lie to him?"

"Only about having a date for tonight."

"And you really think you sold it? 'Cause that was the worst lie I've ever heard."

"You're supposed to be supportive."

"Real friends tell the truth."

"Do I look good?"

"Smokin'." She offers her arm and motions to the club across the street. "Come on. Let's ace this."

"You'll catch me if I fall?"

"Always."

I take her arm and follow her across the street.

———

THE CLUB IS STRAIGHT OUT OF *THE MATRIX*. HIGH CEILINGS, concrete floors, industrial music. The patrons are in a mix of fetish gear and traditional cocktail attire.

It's crowded but not packed. There are a few dozen people on the dance floor, in various states of pre-hookup flirtation, and another two dozen around the bar, on the velvet couches on the edges of the spaces.

We stop at the coat check. The second I slide out of my wool cocoon, I feel naked. Somehow, my snug black dress is both too much and not enough. The harness neckline screams *take me home and tie me up*.

The message is clear, and it's perfect… for Max.

For the other strangers here?

I swallow hard and slip my ticket into my sleek black clutch.

"You want to dance or drink first?" Izzie slides her arm around my waist, the perfect, confident date.

"One drink."

"On you."

"What kind of date are you?"

"The kind who believes in equality."

"Okay, on me." I follow her around the edges of the club, past a row of red loveseats, two friends scoping out their options, a man and a woman making out like there's no tomorrow, a man watching the room carefully.

He's tall and handsome, but he's not Max. His hair is too light, and his clothes are too casual.

I don't know what Max wears on his time off, but I know he wouldn't show up here in jeans.

This place isn't *officially* a bondage club. There are no memberships, Doms on hire, rooms packed with instruments of pain. But there's an off-limits to most upstairs, where people pay for the privilege of watching the action from above.

Or… participating in their own action from above.

The stairs are on the other side of the club and the loft wraps in both directions. Mirrors and red lighting and happy voyeurs.

Is Max up there?

It's too dark to tell.

Izzie taps me on the shoulder. "What are you drinking, sweetness?"

"Sweetness?"

She nods. "Do you prefer angel?"

"Sweetness."

She motions *go on*. "Greyhound."

"Make it two."

"You hate grapefruit juice."

"I'm a gentleman."

"I thought I was paying."

"An enlightened gentleman."

My laugh breaks the tension in my shoulders. She's right. I'm here to have a nice night, dancing with my friend.

I'm not here to stalk Max. Or, uh, set up a situation for Max to stalk me.

After the bartender fixes our drinks, I pay with cash, and I chug half my vodka cranberry. It's not the world's finest cocktail—the vodka is cheap and the grapefruit juice is stale—but it's strong.

Izzie takes small sips as she scans the room. "What about him?"

I follow her gaze to a guy in leather pants and a harness. No shirt. "Aren't you my date?"

"Because you haven't seen him."

"He's wearing a collar."

"And…"

"And…" Fuck. I take another sip, but the alcohol does nothing to stop my blush. "I prefer the other way."

"Oh my god, Opal, you're adorable."

"What?"

"You're shy about wanting Max to tie you up."

"No."

"You're wearing a harness. I don't live under a rock."

"But—"

"And I knew this was a BDSM club. Why do you think I agreed?"

"Because I'm insane and you're a good friend."

"And I want to come and see what's out there."

"What about Jamie?"

"Opal!"

"Did you break up?"

"You agreed."

"Okay, I just… I always support you. Always. But if you want me to lie to him—"

"I'm just dancing."

"I won't lie."

"Except to Max?"

"I'm trying not to lie. To anyone."

"Really, Opes. I'm here to dance and look. That's all."

Are they together? On a break? Broken up?

I take a deep breath and exhale slowly. If she needs time with it before she tells me, I respect that.

If she wants to dance with strangers without judgment, I respect that.

I'm the one here with purpose.

"Oh, three o'clock." She takes another small sip. "He's checking you out."

Sure enough, there's a cute alternative guy at three o'clock. Tight pants, long bangs, leather jacket. But he's not checking *me* out. "He's looking at you."

"He's not."

"He is." I catch the guy's eyes and motion to Izzie.

She looks away with a blush.

"He's shy too."

"We're here to stalk your boyfriend, not find me a date."

"He's not my boyfriend and we're actually—"

"Setting up a situation for him to stalk you, yes. It's very twisted."

"I prefer romantic."

"You would." She glances at the alt guy then returns to the search. "Ah, bingo. Him." A tall guy in a suit.

For a second, I think he's Max, but then he steps into the light, and his face is all wrong.

"He'd tie you up."

"I don't know…"

"What's wrong with him?"

"He's fine."

"And…"

"He's just fine."

She shakes her head. "You're picky."

"Of course. I have the hottest date in the room."

She blushes. "Okay, for that, you have to dance." She finishes her drink in one long chug and offers her hand.

I finish mine, take her hand, follow her into the crowded space.

Even four feet into the dance floor, the energy is different. No one is here to talk. They're here to fuck. The space hums with sex and sweat, leather and plastic.

I close my eyes and sway with the beat. I'm not an excellent dancer, but I love the feeling of freedom that comes with catching the beat.

Everything else fades away. The entire world is me and the music. The entire world is free and easy.

I move with Izzie until I bump into someone. No, run into them.

The alt guy, no longer trying to keep his distance, totally ready to move in on Izzie.

Izzie tries to hide her desire to dance with the new partner, but it's written all over her face.

I motion *go for it*.

"Are you sure?" she calls over the music.

I motion *drink* then point to my phone. "Call me if you need me. Or you go home."

"You'll be okay?"

"I will." I turn to the alt guy. "My friend would love to dance."

He seems to understand, because he moves into Izzie's space right away.

I take the chance to use the restroom, fix my makeup, down a glass of water. When I'm rested and hydrated, I check the dance floor.

The space is packed. I can't see Izzie or Max. Is he here? Upstairs?

At home with another woman?

I bump into someone. A tall man in jeans and a sports jacket. Handsome enough, but not Max.

He asks me to dance.

I accept.

Better to think about something else. Anything else. As long as it's not Max.

For a few minutes, I move in time with the stranger. He keeps his distance, but he still feels too close.

Someone bumps into me. I trip on my heel. Fall into the guy's arms.

He catches me and helps me up. He's a gentleman about it and he's strong and sure, but he feels wrong.

There's nothing odd about it. I don't usually like this kind of guy. I don't like older men. I don't like men in suits. I don't like designer watches or silk ties or eye crinkles.

"Thanks for the dance." I take a step backward, to find my footing, find some space, but I bump into something hard.

Someone.

No, not someone.

Max.

Chapter Twelve

MAX

Opal's big blue eyes go wide. For a moment, she stares with appreciation and wonder. Then her expression shifts.

First, to victory. Then, to frustration.

She says something, but I can't hear her over the music. I can't form a thought. I'm too drawn to her.

The dark makeup around her eyes, the red lips, the long straight hair.

The Opal I saw in my bed. The young woman ready to explore her sexuality and claim what she wants.

Then the adornments picked specifically to drive me out of my mind: the hot pink shoes, the short black dress, the harness crisscrossing her chest.

She's not wearing it for me. This is a busy club. There are dozens of potential dates here. Maybe even her date. Maybe that's the truth.

And who the fuck do I think I am, believing she dresses for me? Is my ego that ridiculous?

But the mix of frustration and desire in her eyes—

How can it be anything else?

She wants me. She hates that she wants me. She hates me for telling her our night together meant nothing.

"What are you doing here?" She moves closer, so her lips are inches from my ear. In her heels, she's the perfect height.

The scent of her shampoo fills my nostrils. Citrus and honey. And something else, some mix of soap and Opal. It takes every ounce of my restraint to keep my hands at my sides. "The same thing you are."

She scoffs, not believing me or realizing we're both full of shit.

"Where's your date?" I ask.

"They wanted to dance with someone else."

"You don't mind?"

"We didn't have the right spark."

My stomach settles. She's not going home with someone else. "Are they here?"

"I'm here to dance. So we can dance or you can go."

It's a bluff, but I'm not willing to call her on it. The risk is too great. I can't watch her dance with someone else. I can't watch some man put his hands on her skin, whisper in her ear, offer to tie her to his bed.

She wants to learn. She wants to experience this. She isn't going to stop because I've said no.

Either she's here to drive me wild, or she's here to find someone else.

Both, maybe.

I tell myself it's the latter, that she doesn't care, that I need to release her now, but I don't believe it.

Leave. Do the smart thing. Let her go.

My body disobeys my command. I'm too tired. It's been too long.

Staying here, in New York, surrounded by Raul's work, his space, his business—

There's no break. Only my time with her.

And that isn't enough.

I need more.

I need every fucking drop of sunshine.

I move toward her reflexively. One hand goes to her lower back. The other rests on her shoulder. I brush her hair aside, let my fingers curl around her neck. "Let's."

Her breath hitches as I pull her closer.

Her hands slip under my suit jacket. Curl around my waist.

I've never been a dancer. I've never learned the steps or the gestures.

But I know how to lead.

And Opal knows how to follow.

She shifts with the slightest movements, melting into me the way she did.

She's every bit as pliant and responsive here.

I close my eyes and try to sink into the music.

For a moment, I'm there, dancing with any other woman at any other club. Then I smell her citrus shampoo and I'm here with her, desperate to rip her clothes off and lock her in my castle.

Far away from anyone who can hurt her.

I pull her closer.

She rolls her hips with the beat, grinding against me, driving me mad with the perfect friction.

Why did I wear a designer suit? I should have worn a suit of armor. Or a chastity belt.

Whatever it takes to keep my slacks zipped.

She turns and melts into me again. Her ass against my pelvis, her back against my chest, her head falling into the crook of my neck.

Again, my hands disobey my command. One goes to her hips. The other wraps around her neck.

She gasps and arches into me. "Max."

This is beyond a casual dance. This is beyond an inappropriate dance.

This is completely and totally over the line.

And I don't care.

I need her warmth, her groan, her bliss.

I reach for some hit of sense, but nothing comes. My body is too tuned to hers. My brain is too tired.

All these nights, fighting with myself, trying to avoid the ugly thoughts in my head. I'm out of willpower.

I pull her closer.

She rocks against me, grinding with perfect slow circles, driving me out of my fucking mind again and again.

It's too much. It's not enough.

I need to be inside her.

I need to taste her cunt.

I need to come immediately.

"Let's talk." Finally, I find a hint of sense, but I lose it just as quickly. "Upstairs."

She turns and hooks her arms around my neck. "Upstairs?"

I nod.

She stares into my eyes. For a long moment, she stays close, her lips inches from mine, her posture screaming *kiss me*.

I haven't kissed her. I haven't kissed anyone new in a long time.

Hell, I haven't kissed anyone in a long time.

But I'm desperate to claim every inch of Opal.

Get a fucking grip. She's beyond off-limits.

There's no willpower left in the reservoir, nothing but a deep, endless need to touch her.

I pull back, hoping the loss of contact will allow blood to return to my brain.

It doesn't.

I press my palm into her lower back and lead her through the crowded space. The bouncer at the staircase nods with recognition and unhooks the velvet rope.

Opal's fingers trail against the railing as she moves up the stairs. Her hips sway. Her dress rides up her ass.

Pink.

She's wearing something pink under her dress.

The same shade as her shoes.

Another soft, sweet pair?

Immediately, the image forms in my mind. Opal Pierce, in only her shoes and panties, my tie around her wrists.

Fuck.

I follow her up the stairs.

She looks around curiously, noting the semi-secluded space.

A group of friends sits in the corner of the balcony, watching the action as they sip a two-hundred-dollar bottle of Belvedere.

A couple trading dirty promises on a velvet love seat.

Two people making out against the wall.

And then my seat. The couch hidden behind a sheer curtain.

"Here." I lead her past the red lace. "Do you want a drink?"

She shakes her head and takes a seat.

I slide across from her, but it's barely any distance. A foot maybe. And I have a better view of her.

The red lips, the curious eyes, the part of her thighs.

The harness covering her chest—

Instantly, my blood returns to my cock. There's no way I can have this conversation in this state.

But what the fuck can I say?

She plucks one of the bottles of water from the table, unscrews the cap, takes greedy sips. "Thanks." She offers me the other, copying my gesture from last time.

But there isn't a last time, because there isn't a this time or a next time.

I'm here to end this infatuation.

I try to find the words, some way to start, but it's all bullshit.

"You should stay hydrated." She takes another sip, caps her bottle, sets it on the low table.

"I appreciate the advice." The water is too warm. It does nothing to cool my temperature or lower my heart rate.

She looks up at me, curious and frustrated. "Are you going to tell me why you happened to be here tonight?"

"Would you believe me?"

"Would you believe I told you the name of the club on accident?"

"No."

She raises a brow *no*. "Then why are you here? If the night didn't matter?"

"You know why."

"Do I?"

"Opal—"

"I'm aware of my name. If you're here to feed me more bullshit, I'll go." She taps the leather couch with her bright pink nails. "I respected your wishes, every one of them. If you're so twisted over the possibility of me with someone else—"

"I can't stop thinking about you."

"How do you think I feel?"

She can't be as fixated as I am. She's young and beautiful. There are a million men who would kill for the chance to teach her.

She has her issues, sure, but she's sunshine.

She's not darkness.

Fuck. I'm doing it again. The same way I did to Raul.

She's beautiful and bright.

She still hurts.

Everyone does.

"I don't want things to be awkward," she says. "At school. But that's impossible now, isn't it?"

There's a way around it. A way to make this right for her. For both of us. "What if you have to choose?"

"Choose what?"

"This or that. Sex or school?" I swallow hard. I'm not prepared for the answer. Not as a man or an artist or a person with the ability to resist someone. "No more lessons. No more help with your project."

She nods, understanding.

"If you could only have one, which would it be?"

Chapter Thirteen

MAX

"Do you doubt my answer?" Opal asks.
I try to tap into my willpower, but the well is empty. "No."
"I want to be with you again. I want to learn from you here."
"There are other men who will teach you this."
"I don't want them."
My stomach settles. My pulse races.
"I want you. And if you followed me here, you want me too."
"I do."
"Then why not?"
"It's wrong."
"Do you care?"
Not as much as I should. I swallow hard.
"What if this is part of my self-discovery? What if I need someone who can help me tie my sexuality and art together?"
"Do you?"
"Does it matter?"
"Yes."
"I don't know if I need it, but I want it."
Fuck, I want to say yes. "It has to be on my terms."

"What rule have I broken?"

She's right. I'm the one who suddenly took over as her professor. I'm the one who called our night together nothing. I'm the one who followed her here.

Even so—

"On my terms, Opal," I say.

She nods *go on*.

"Never on campus or during the week."

"In your office?"

"From the moment you arrive to the start of class Monday morning."

"All weekend?"

"All weekend."

"What if I run into you outside of school?"

"Pretend I'm only your professor."

"I want a way to contact you during the week," she says.

I should say no, but I can't resist the possibility. "Only texts."

"No calls?"

"Only if there's an emergency."

She nods. "I can do that." She uncrosses and recrosses her legs. "For how long?"

"Until one of us says when."

"That's it?"

"An easy out, anytime."

"If I say I'm done, you won't follow me on my next date?"

I want to promise that, but I don't trust myself. "I'll respect your wishes."

"Okay." She offers her hand. "It's a deal."

I take it. Shake.

It is a deal. We need to celebrate it. And I need to make sure she's ready to take orders. Here and elsewhere.

"Stand," I say.

She does.

"What are you wearing under that?"

"Underwear."

"Show me."

She pulls her dress up her thighs, showing a hint of her deep pink panties.

"Take them off."

She slides her panties to her ankles and kicks them off her feet.

"Come here."

She takes a step toward me. Another. Another.

I bring my hands to her hips and turn her around.

She gasps as I pull her into my lap. "Fuck." She rocks against me. "You're hard."

Very.

"Max. Please."

"Please?"

"I want to touch you."

"No."

A whine falls from her lips.

"Hands on the cushion."

She places her palms on the leather cushions.

"Keep them there, or I'll stop. Understand?"

"Yes."

"Spread your legs."

"Here?"

A demanding tone drops into my voice. "You beckoned me here."

"Yes."

"What did you imagine happening?"

"Everything."

"Specifically."

"Your hands on my skin, under my dress, on the dance floor. The two of us in some secluded corner, fucking against the wall. You, dragging me back to your place."

"Did you touch yourself?"

"Yes."
"How many times?"
"Once. But I came three times."
"When?"
"Last night."
"Was that the first time you thought of me?"
"No. Every night, since our first text."
Fuck. "Have you been with anyone else?"
"No."
"Do you want anyone else?"
"No."
"Good girl."
A purr falls from her lips.
"This is something you imagined?"
"Yes."
"But you're scared we'll be caught?"
"Yes."
"We won't."
"Someone could see," she says.
"Or hear. But there won't be trouble. Not here."
"What if we were somewhere else?"
"I'll protect you."
"You promise?"
"Always."
She nods with understanding.
"I won't ask twice again."
She pushes her knees apart.

I find the zipper of her dress and pull it down an inch at a time.

Opal groans as I roll her dress to her waist, exposing her breasts. She arches her back, rocking into me, rolling her ass against my pelvis.

My body begs me to relent, to toss her dress aside and fuck her right here, right now.

But I won't. Not tonight. I need to test her.

I need to test myself.

To make sure I can play by these rules.

To give my brain a chance to seize control from my dick.

Opal rocks her ass against my cock and my thoughts scatter. She feels good. Too fucking good. I need all of it.

But I need to wait too. To wait until it's nearly too much to take, until it is too much to take, until I want her more than I've ever wanted anything.

I'm already close—

In every fucking definition of the word.

This is too much friction.

I can't toy with her the way I want, for as long as I want, but this isn't the time or the place for that.

I cup her breasts with my hands, rolling my thumbs over her nipples.

She groans, rocking against me, digging her nails into the leather.

I bring my lips to her neck. Tease her with hard kisses and soft scrapes of my teeth.

Again and again, until she's panting—

Until I'm at the fucking brink—

Then I whisper the words I'm desperate to hear, "Touch yourself."

She lifts her right hand and goes straight to the spot where she needs stimulation. No teasing, no toying, only steady strokes of her index finger against her clit.

Her head rolls back. Her left hand lifts.

I wrap my fingers around her wrist and hold her hand against the couch.

She gasps with a mix of surprise and delight. She wants to be under my control. She wants to be mine.

And, fuck, I want her to be mine.

I grip her a little tighter; I bite her a little harder; I toy a little rougher.

She melts into me, groaning into the space as she rubs herself.

Again and again.

Then she's there, tugging at the leather, groaning my name as she comes.

It's the best sound I've heard.

I need it again.

I need it forever.

I need it now.

But this is a test of my restraint too.

I wait for her to catch her breath, then I release her arm, right her dress, help her to her feet.

She turns around, so we're eye to eye. "Is that… all?"

"Was it not enough?"

"Nothing would be enough."

Fuck, how does she know the perfect thing to say? "For tonight."

She nods with understanding. "I should probably go back to my friend."

"I don't want you dancing with someone else."

"It's just dancing."

"What if I was dancing with someone?"

"I wouldn't like it."

"This is a relationship," I say. "We both have terms."

"That's fair… because it's sexual." She bends to pick up her panties.

I take them. Slip them into my pocket.

Her chest heaves with her inhale. "You should ask too."

"I don't ask."

"Here, maybe. But elsewhere, you should ask."

"May I keep your underwear?"

"Yes." Her eyes meet mine. "I like you, Max. I like this. I

understand what it is and I want that. But I have three brothers. I don't need another one."

"I'm going to protect you."

"As a… fuck buddy?"

Not exactly. "You're asking me to teach you, to introduce you to this type of play?"

She nods.

"I'm going to protect you here. Places like this. With other men, men with bad intentions."

"Or women."

Does she sleep with women too? "With anyone."

"As a…"

"Submissive."

The word makes her cheeks flush. "Is it official?"

"Do you want to sign a contract?"

"Do you have one made up?"

"I can."

"I'll think about it." She gathers her purse. "I guess I'll go then…"

"I'll call a car."

"I mean it, Max. I have three brothers."

"As your partner, I'm making sure you get home okay. It's not negotiable." It's not exactly ace aftercare, but it's something. I'm rusty. It's been too long.

"I'm here with someone."

"Your date?" That was a real story?

"A friend."

"We can say goodbye to your friend together. Or you can text after I put you in a car. Your choice."

"I'll text her." My relief must be obvious, because she laughs. "I could be sleeping with her."

"Are you?"

"No. But I could."

"Do you sleep with women?"

"Not yet." She smiles, daring me to respond with jealousy. Or maybe with some idiotic *girl on girl is hot* frat boy shit.

"No one else while we're together."

"I understand," she says.

"It's been a while for me. I can send a recent test."

"How long?"

"A few months. I was with someone, but we were… growing apart."

"A girlfriend?"

"Yes."

"A serious one?"

"Three years."

She presses her lips together. "I haven't been with anyone since we started talking. But right before that… I slept with my ex. We were safe, but I can get a recent test."

"Are you on birth control?"

"The pill."

"If this is a long-term arrangement, we can take steps."

"How long term?"

"Until I leave."

"When do you leave?"

I don't know, but I know the plan. "After the semester."

"That's only a few weeks."

"Six weeks." It doesn't sound like enough. I want an eternity with her. But it's what we have. "We can try without a condom. If you're comfortable."

"I'm comfortable." She presses her lips together. "If it's safe."

"You can change your mind at any point," I say. "About this. Or anything else."

"Just say cranberry?"

"Or 'no.' Or 'I'm not sure.' Whatever fits the situation."

"But I won't talk you out of walking me out?"

"It's one of my terms," I say. "Making sure you get home safe."

"You have a lot of terms."

"Is that a problem?"

"No. Just not what you project. It's an interesting contrast." She offers her hand, the left. "I need to get my coat."

I take her hand, lead her downstairs, to the coat check, then outside.

The air is cold, freezing, but it's not enough to cool my temperature.

I need to put her in a car now, before I give in to my desire to invite myself to go home with her.

I hail the cab across the street.

"A cab, really? That's so old school." She laughs and follows me across the street.

I help her into the car. "I won't see you again this weekend."

Her lips curl into a pout. "Oh."

"But we'll do this again Friday."

"The art lessons?"

"Then the others."

She smiles. "Good."

"I have two assignments for you."

She nods, ready.

"One, if you really do want to combine these lessons, I want to see it, in visual form."

"Fair."

"And, two, don't touch yourself until you see me."

She pouts again. "All week?"

"All week. I want your next orgasm to be on my lips."

Chapter Fourteen

MAX

I play by the same terms.
 Every night, I think of Opal, I resist fucking myself, I struggle to sleep.
Every day, the test gets harder.
Harder.
Nearly impossible.
On Thursday, when we trade test results, when she tells me she wants to fuck without a condom—
I barely make it.
Friday, I'm ready to burst and utterly incapable of concentrating. I barely make it through my work.
I clear the office.
I make the space comfortable for Opal.
I even make it through our lesson without touching her.
Then, right as she slips her sketchbook into her backpack, I start.
"Did you follow my instructions?" I bring my lips to her neck.
She leans into the touch. "Yes."
"Was it hard?"
"Miserable."

"For me too."

"You did too?"

"It's only fair." I run my lips over her neck, then I pull back. Straighten. "Stand."

She does.

"Take off your sweater."

She looks around the quiet office, deems it empty enough, tosses her bright blue sweater over her head.

She stands tall and proud in a camisole and jeans.

She's already barefoot. She's comfortable working that way.

But this—

Fuck, I'm not going to last.

"The shirt," I say.

She pulls it over her head.

"The bra."

She reaches behind her back, undoes the hook, lets the garment fall to her feet.

Opal Pierce, in my office, in only her jeans.

Fuck, she's gorgeous.

I bring one hand to her lower back and pull her body into mine. I don't kiss her. Not on the lips. Not yet.

I bring my mouth to the crook of her jaw.

She shudders as I kiss a line down her neck. Then back up, to the line of her jaw.

"On your knees," I demand.

"Oh."

"Is that a problem?"

"No."

"Do you have a sensitive gag reflex?"

She reaches for me. Grabs my waist. "No. I don't think so."

"I won't be gentle." It's not true, exactly. It's our first time. I need to ease her into it. But I want her to feel this, to feel lost in this.

I offer my hand. When she takes it, I help her onto her knees.

"Have you done this?"

"Yes."

"Rough?"

"No."

My shoulders settle. My cock whines. I want to be the first to really claim her this way.

I'm too hard.

Too eager.

But that's better for the first time.

Easier for her.

I cup her cheek with my palm. Run my thumb over her lip.

She waits, patiently, for me to slip my digit into her mouth.

She looks up at me as she sucks softly.

Then harder.

Fuck.

This is enough.

How am I going to survive ten seconds in her sweet, wet mouth?

I press the pad of my thumb into her tongue. I savor the feel of her for another moment, then I pull back. "Next time, I'll bind your wrists. This time, hands at your sides."

She nods. Watches as I undo my belt, button, zipper.

I push my boxers aside.

My cock springs free.

Opal's eyes go wide. Because she wants me? Because she's not usually this close?

I don't know. I don't care.

As long as I have her interest.

Her need.

Her obsession.

I'm already too far gone, and I don't care about that either.

I bring my hand to the back of her head. She settles into the posture, melting into me, falling into that perfect place.

"Open your mouth," I say.

She does.

I bring her closer. Until her lips brush my cock.

Soft. A hint.

Then harder.

Enough to drive me out of my fucking mind.

I savor the perfect pressure for a moment, then I press my palm into the back of her head, driving her mouth over me.

Fuck.

It's been a long time.

And this is Opal—

The woman haunting my dreams. My sexual fantasies. My every-kind of fantasies.

I knot my hand in her hair, holding her in place, then I pull back and shift into her pretty pink mouth again.

Slowly at first.

Then a little faster.

A little harder.

Until it's the pressure and rhythm I need.

Her warm softness envelops me again and again.

I push a little deeper.

Until she's struggling to take it.

Then I bring my hand to her chest. Toy with her nipple as I fuck her pretty mouth.

She groans against my cock.

It's too much for her. She won't last.

But I won't either.

And this is what I promised—

I close my eyes and give in to the sensation.

Her soft, warm mouth.

Her pert nipple.

Her groan against my skin.

I open my eyes. Take in the sight.

This gorgeous, leggy brunette, in nothing but her jeans, her pretty pink lips wrapped around my cock.

I come on the spot.

Pleasure rolls through me. Hard, heavy waves. My cock pulses. My hand knots in her hair. My lips part with a groan.

"Fuck, Opal." I hold her against me as I spill into her mouth.

She takes every drop. Waits for me to release her. Swallows hard.

I right my slacks, then I offer my hand and help her to her feet. "Too much?"

"No."

"Could you take more?"

"Could you go again?"

"Another time?"

"With practice." She straightens, tall and proud and perfect. "I'd be happy to practice."

"Would you?"

She nods. "I could drop by your office Tuesday. I'll be in the neighborhood anyway. Dinner with my brother."

"Really?"

"You don't believe me?"

I do. That's the problem.

"We meet at six thirty. How about I come by at five thirty?"

"The place will be crowded."

"You have blinds."

I do.

Fuck, if Raul was alive, he'd kill me for turning her down. A gorgeous young woman offering to drop by my place anytime to suck me off?

What the fuck happened to my life?

How the fuck can I consider saying no to that?

"Tuesday," I say.

She beams.

"Keep the top off." I pick up her coat and hang it over her shoulders. "I want you walking home like this."

"Home?"

"To my place."

"For the rest of the night?"

"Unless you have a problem with that."

"Are you going to fuck me?"

"Yes."

"You promise?"

"No."

She pouts, but she still cinches her coat, gathers her things, and follows me to the elevator.

Chapter Fifteen

OPAL

Even though it's a cool night, the six-block walk to Max's apartment sets me on fire. Knowing I'm topless under my coat—

Knowing he wants me like this—

Fuck.

I don't notice the streets we walk, the nearby buildings, the other people in the apartment. Only the feeling of his hand against my back, pressing my coat into my bare skin.

We stop on a high floor. He leads me down the hallway to a corner apartment.

Inside, the space is sparse and modern. A one-bedroom. Maybe two. Barely decorated.

"Are you staying here?" I ask.

"Until the semester ends." He slides his suit jacket off his shoulders and rolls his sleeves to his elbows. He stops behind me and runs his finger over the neckline of my wool coat. "It's a short-term rental."

"You were staying at the hotel?"

"When I first arrived."

He invited me into his space that night. And he's doing it

again. It means something, but I don't have enough blood in my brain to put the pieces together.

He traces the neckline again. "Did you eat dinner?"

"Yes. You?"

"Before our session." He leans down and presses his lips to my neck. "Do you want something to drink?"

"Water."

He places a hard kiss on my neck. Then it's the scrape of his teeth.

My body hums. I need him. I need him now. I need what he promised.

This wait is agony.

Perfect agony.

"Your wish is my command." He pulls back and moves to the sink.

It's only a few steps. The main room is small, but with the lack of furniture, it seems spacious. There's only a small table and two chairs and they're against the wide window. "For a Californian, you pick places with great views."

The city is alive against the night sky.

It's beautiful.

Perfect.

He fills two glasses and hands one to me. "Raul picked this place. Company housing."

That makes more sense.

"He loved the city."

"Does that make it hard… being here?"

"Sometimes." He brings the glass to his lips and takes a long sip. "It would be hard no matter what."

"Do you want to talk about it?"

"Do you?"

Kind of. And not at all.

I want to talk to Max for hours.

And I want to fuck him for hours.

"If you do," I say.

"But you'd rather I put my mouth to other uses?"

"You promised."

"I know."

"Are you... ready to go again?"

He smiles.

"What?"

"You ask often."

"I'm curious."

"About male biology?"

"About how many times you can fuck me in one night."

His pupils dilate. "Is that a dare?"

"Maybe."

"Bad girl."

My cheeks flush.

He finishes his drink. Sets it on the counter. Waits for me to finish mine.

When I do, he peels my fingers from the glass and sets it aside.

He moves behind me again, runs his fingers over the wool neckline of my coat again, presses his lips to my neck again.

But he doesn't undo my button.

He doesn't slide his hand between my legs.

He doesn't order me onto my knees.

He teases me with the soft brush of his lips, again and again.

"Do you want to see the rest of the place?" he asks.

"Please."

He presses his palm into my lower back and leads me around the corner to a narrow hallway, past three doors (two on the left, one on the right) to the sliding glass entrance to the balcony.

He pulls the door open and motions *after you*.

I step outside onto the red tile. The view is even better here. Skyscrapers with pockets of yellow light in every direction. And the deep blue water of the Hudson.

Fuck, I'm breathless.

Then he steps outside and I'm hot as hell too.

"I come here often," he says. "And I think about you."

"What do you think?"

"The wonder in your gorgeous blue eyes as you take in the view. The way you marvel at the city and art and me."

My cheeks flush.

"And this…" He looks me in the eyes as he runs his fingers over my neck. "Winding you tight with anticipation. As tight as I can, until you're not sure if you can take it."

"I am."

"This is nothing."

"Max—"

"Do you have an objection?"

"No."

"You know how to object?"

"Yes."

He traces the line of my coat all the way to the top button. Slowly, he undoes it. Then the second. The third.

The sides fall apart, revealing me to him.

It's different than it was in his office. We're in his apartment. On his balcony.

Somehow, in his space and on view to the rest of the world too.

And fuck, the desire in his eyes—

My sex pangs.

I need him.

I need him now.

I need him forever.

"Please." The word falls off my lips.

"Not yet." He steps behind me and helps me out of my coat, the same way he's done a million times. "Wait here. I'll hang it on the rack."

"Please—"

"Then come inside with me." He leads me through the door, back around the hallway, all the way to the coat rack at the entrance.

Every step winds me tighter. How is that possible? He's not even touching me and I'm on fire. I'm totally and completely desperate for him.

For more.

"You look good here." He cups my cheek with his palm.

"Your apartment?"

"The city." He looks around the space, studying it as if he's never seen it before. "And in my apartment."

"Thank you."

He runs his thumb over my temple. For a long moment, he stares into my eyes, then he leans closer.

Closer.

Close enough to kiss me.

But he doesn't. Not on the lips, at least.

He goes straight to the corner of my jaw. Kisses a line down my neck, along my shoulder, over my collarbone.

Then lower.

His lips close around my nipple.

He sucks with soft pressure.

Then harder.

The scrape of his teeth.

Fuck. The tension in my sex winds tighter. Tighter. Almost too tight to bear.

I'm on the edge already.

Is it possible to come like this?

It feels all too possible.

My thoughts scatter as he scrapes his teeth against me again.

I reach for him. Get the soft fabric of his shirt. The smooth fibers of his hair. It's too short for me to grab, but there's something satisfying about that too.

Something pure and perfect.

"Max—" My fingers curl into his upper back, but the cotton of his shirt is between us. It's too much. Too many layers.

He responds with a sharp flick of his teeth. Another. Another.

Then he moves to my other nipple and teases me just as mercilessly.

Again and again.

Winding me tighter and tighter.

Closer and closer.

How can I be close from this?

I need more.

And I need him to keep doing this, forever.

"Please." I tug at his shirt.

He flicks his tongue against me. Then he pulls back. Straightens. Undoes the knot of his tie.

Fuck.

But he doesn't use the tie.

No. He unbuckles his belt instead. "Hands."

I place my hands in front of me.

He loops the leather around my wrists. Tests the knot. Deems it just right.

Then the same pattern. Only slower and infinitely more torturous.

His lips against my jaw.

A line down my neck. Over my collarbone. Down my chest.

His lips around my nipple.

That soft, perfect suction.

Then harder.

The sharp scrape of his teeth.

I reach for him. Catch the belt.

Fuck. It's too much. I can't take more.

But I can't ask him to stop either.

I need this. All this. Forever.

He toys with me again and again.

Until I'm dizzy with pleasure.

Then, finally, he brings his hand to my jeans. He undoes the button. The zipper. He peels the jeans off my hips and leaves them at mid-thigh.

Then the panties.

He presses a kiss to my pelvis.

Then it's the soft brush of his lips against me.

Fuck.

My eyes close.

My fingers dig into my palms.

He brushes against me again, a little firmer.

Firmer.

Fuck.

It's enough.

The tension in me winds to a fever pitch. With the next brush of his lips, I come.

My sex pulses.

Pleasure rolls through my body. My toes curl. My thighs shake. My knees threaten to collapse.

But he has me.

He catches me. Stands. Lifts me into his arms.

Max carries me to his bed.

It's fast and it's dark. I can't see much of his room. Only the mirrored closet, the silk sheets, the clean hardwood floor.

And Max, flipping me over, unbuttoning his slacks.

He pushes my thighs apart.

They catch on my jeans.

The feel of being bound—by my bottoms and the belt around my wrists—winds me tighter. Already, I'm close again.

Already, I'm humming with need.

For him.

Like everything.

And like this.

Especially like this.

Max digs his fingers into my hip and he drives into me.

There's no warning, no warmup, no tease.

No barrier.

His flesh against mine.

All of him against all of me.

He goes hard and deep.

It's intense, but I stretch to take him.

He pulls back and drives into me again.

And again.

Every thrust pushes me closer.

And closer.

Then his nails scrape my skin. One hand on my hip. The other drawing a long line down my back.

Down.

Then up.

Then back to my hips.

He holds me in place as he drives into me.

Again and again.

Hard enough, my thighs shake.

And the belt digs into my stomach.

But the hurt only winds me tighter.

Tighter.

There—

With his next thrust, I come. My sex pulses around him, pulling him closer, taking him deeper.

And then he's there with me, pulsing inside me, rocking through his orgasm, groaning my name as he comes.

It's perfect.

Everything.

I'm his.

And he knows exactly how to work me. Exactly how to bend and pose and stretch me.

Exactly how to please me.

He lingers there for one perfect moment, then he pulls back and fixes his clothes.

He kneels to help me out of my boots, socks, jeans, panties.

He sits next to me on the bed, turns me over, undoes the belt.

I lie there, on the silk sheets, satisfied and spent.

And then he's there next to me, his arms around me, his chest against my back, his breath against my neck.

"Too much?" he asks.

"Perfect."

"You were perfect." He presses his lips to my neck. "You always are."

My cheeks flush.

My chest too.

It's a strange reaction to a compliment, after all that. And it's too soon to say, really. We've only been together a few times.

But it's true for me too. "You too."

I'm not sure how long we lie together. It could be five minutes or five hours. Time has no meaning. Only the perfect feeling of his breath on my neck, the perfect pressure of his chest against my back, his arm around my stomach.

Eventually, he presses another kiss to my jaw and he pulls back. He moves into another room. Returns with a glass of water.

"Careful." He takes my hand and helps me to a seated position. "It's easy to get dizzy."

It is.

He wraps my fingers around the water. Watches as I drink the glass. With sips. Then gulps. "Do you need more?"

"I'm okay."

"You can stay."

I can? But for how long? Another hour? The entire night? All weekend?

Forever?

I want to stay.

I want to stay forever.

But that's dangerous.

That's not our arrangement.

And, besides, I told Simon I'd be home by two. I don't want to explain this to him. "I should head home. My brother is expecting me."

"I'll call a car."

"No. I've got it."

"I insist."

"Okay. If you insist."

He smiles.

My heart thuds against my chest. He has the world's most beautiful smile.

Max pulls out his cell and he…

Calls.

He actually calls to arrange a cab. I must be staring, because he raises a brow.

"Yes?" he asks.

"Who calls?"

"It's faster." He kneels in front of me, tender and patient, and presses his lips to my knees. Then he helps me into my socks.

He dresses me slowly and carefully, one item at a time, then he helps me up, walks me to the door.

I gather my things.

He insists on walking me out, of course.

And helping me into the car.

I don't object. I'm still in a daze. It's normal, I guess. After sex. And after this.

"Text me when you get home." He pushes the door closed.

"Okay."

He nods good night.

The car pulls away. I watch the city whiz by the windows, one neighborhood at a time. It's a beautiful night, as clear as it gets here, and just the right temperature for the window to stay open a crack.

At home, Simon is asleep. I shower, climb into my pajamas, text Max about my safe arrival.

And then I fall into a perfect, safe sleep.

Chapter Sixteen

OPAL

All weekend, I think of Max.

On Tuesday, I take him up on his offer.

I drop by his office.

And drop to my knees.

But he doesn't finish there. He picks me up, bends me over his desk, fucks me senseless.

It's rough and soft and perfect.

And I'm dizzy and happy and spent. I'm in a cloud as he helps me into my clothes and walks me to my brother's office.

A perfect, happy cloud of sex and affection.

Completely and totally blown away by the whirlwind that is my brother Liam.

Fuck.

Liam shoots me a *you fucked up* smile. His blue eyes shine with evil glee. "Who's your friend?" His satisfaction is palpable.

After all, he lives and dies to make everyone's life difficult. And here I am, handing him a silver bullet.

Shit.

"Your much older friend?" he asks. "How old are you, anyway?"

"Liam! That's a rude question!" I say.

"You should hear my next question," he says. "Also a number."

I shoot him a *stop* look.

He returns a *hell no*.

Max watches carefully. "Max Morrison." He offers his hand.

My brother shakes. "Where's that been?"

"LIAM!" My cheeks flame.

"Kidding." Liam shoots me a look that says *absolutely not kidding*. "What is your friend doing here?"

"We were just—" There's not enough blood in my brain. I don't know how to deal with my difficult brother.

"Just fucked." He looks us both up and down and shakes his head. "You gotta learn to hide it better."

"Working," I say.

"My work makes me blush too." Liam makes a show of fanning himself. "Quarterly budgets. What's sexier than that?"

"LIAM!"

"You can say it as many times as you want," Liam says. "It won't help you sell your story to Simon." He turns to someone behind us and smiles even wider. "Speak of the devil."

Simon, thankfully, ignores Liam. "Thai?"

"Yes, please," I say.

"Is your friend going to join?" Liam asks.

Somehow, my blush deepens.

Simon raises a brow. "Your friend?"

Max turns to my brother and introduces himself.

Is it obvious we had sex?

Fuck, it's obvious, isn't it?

"My friend too. Quite a coincidence, actually," Liam says.

"You're friends with Opal's professor?" Simon asks.

HOW DOES HE KNOW THAT?

"I work around the corner," Max says.

"He's meeting me for dinner. So why don't we join forces, huh?" Liam asks.

Simon shoots me a suspicious look.

"I don't want to intrude," Max says.

"Nonsense," Liam says. "We love company. I'll call Briar."

"Yes. Please." I need the buffer. And the girl talk support. "Right away."

He taps a few lines into his text. "She'll meet us there," Liam says. "The place around the corner?"

"Perfect." Simon nods with certainty. The certainty he's onto important information. Like a bloodhound for secrets. My secrets. "If that works for you, Mr. Morrison?"

"Max, please," Max says. "If you don't mind a boring dinner with your professor, Opal."

Liam scoffs *who are you trying to fool?*

"Of course not," I say.

Dinner with my brothers and my fuck buddy.

Great.

Really fucking great.

Chapter Seventeen

OPAL

How can five minutes feel like an eternity? Every second of the walk to the Thai restaurant is excruciating. My ears are ringing. My pulse is pounding.

Everything is a blur of voices. Liam's enthusiasm. Simon's suspicion. Max's stoicism.

Even as we take our seats at the restaurant, stare at our menus, order.

I don't notice my surroundings until Briar joins us.

"Hey, Opal." She nods *hello*. "Can you do me a favor?" She motions toward the direction of the bathroom. "Help me with a fashion emergency."

She's in a normal post-work outfit. A sheath dress and studded ankle boots. She looks fantastic, as usual. Her purple hair is in a perfect neat line. Her eye makeup is enough to say *badass yet professional* and bring out the flecks of green in her grey-green eyes. And her wine lipstick?

Well, it's a little worn, I guess, but there's no emergency.

"Opal." She nods again. Motions for my hand.

"She wants to talk shit with you in the bathroom," Liam says.

She shoots Liam a cutting look.

He smiles, effortless and charming and happy to frustrate her.

She tries to fight a smile, but she fails. Even now, after years working with him, and months of dating (months of engagement, even), she loves to hate his antics. Not that she admits it.

"No. It's a private matter," Briar says.

"If this is about your panties—" Liam winks.

She shoots him an even more *shut the fuck up* look.

"Excuse me." I take Briar's hand and slide out of my seat. Thankfully, we're at a table for six, not a booth. Less thankfully, we're way in the corner, and the restaurant is basically empty. There's no cover. No buffer.

Only Simon's suspicion and Liam's desire to make everyone's life difficult.

Briar leads me around the corner, into the single-stall bathroom. It's a familiar space—Simon and I have been here many times—but it feels strange at the moment.

Wide mirror, black tile, floral wallpaper. Is that a lotus blossom? Or some other flower with an association with Southeast Asia?

It's a pretty pattern. Pink and gold on black.

"Are you okay?" Briar locks the door. "You're spacey."

"I'm always spacey."

"Not this spacey," she says.

"Liam invited himself."

"Liam always invites himself." She brushes a purple lock behind her ear and looks me in the eyes.

It's too much. I shift my gaze to the mirror, to my still flushed cheeks and still dazed expression. "Do you have lipstick?"

She shoots me a look similar to the one she offered Liam. *Do you really think I believe this bullshit?* But, still, she fishes a tube from her small black purse and places it in my palm. "It won't look as dramatic on you."

Tempting Teacher

She has a softer complexion than I do. And my hair is a lot darker than her natural color.

I try to focus on the lipstick. The perfect application, the pout, the differences between our coloring.

She doesn't buy it, but she waits until I'm finished, until I place the lipstick in her palm to press.

"Do you know what Liam told me?" she asks.

"Something about how he yearns for you."

"After that?"

"Something else about how he yearns for you."

"He said you're fucking your professor."

Fuck.

"I thought he was full of shit, but—"

"It's not—"

"You don't have to convince me."

"I don't?"

"A little." She looks me in the eyes again. "It's not smart."

"Liam was your boss."

"That wasn't smart either."

"It worked out."

"It doesn't always. And people still whisper about me."

"A lot?"

"Enough."

That's bullshit, but it's not a battle I can fight. I have to convince her of this. "No one knows."

"No one?"

"Only my best friend."

"You mean I'm not your best friend?"

"You sound like Liam."

"It's awful, I know." She gives me a moment of reprieve. Looks to the mirror to fix her lipstick. "What did you tell her?"

"Izzie?"

She nods.

"Well, I didn't. She put it together. And that was before he…

we had a night together, before he was my professor. And I, uh, didn't want to let it go."

"A Pierce through and through."

"I don't think Simon will high-five me for it."

"Does Simon high-five?"

"You know what I mean."

"I do. But, uh, Opal… it's really obvious."

"It is?"

"Between the blush and the way you're staring at Max… if you don't have a better story—"

"Would you believe a crush?"

"Maybe."

"Would Simon?"

"He's your brother."

"It's not… I'm the one who pursued him."

"I'm not judging."

"At all?"

She shakes her head. "I worry. You're like my kid sister."

"You hate your sister."

"I don't hate her. We disagree about our parents."

"Still—"

"You're like my kid sister I adore. Is that better?"

"Yes. Thanks."

She smiles. "You sound like Liam now."

"He's my half-brother."

Her smile widens.

"Is it that obvious?"

"It's obvious there's something."

"Will you tell Liam it's only a crush?"

"Yes."

"Really?"

"Absolutely. And if Liam asked me to keep a secret from you, I'd honor that too."

"Has he?"

She mimes zipping her lips.

"It's Liam. He doesn't have secrets."

She doesn't agree, but she doesn't press it either. "What happened with your professor?"

"Max? Well… you swear you won't tell anyone?"

"I swear."

I tell her everything.

―――

When we're done, Briar is as red as I am. And as sure we need to keep this from my brother. "You can't tell Simon."

"I know."

"The crush is plausible. He's handsome."

"Isn't he?"

She smiles. "And he seems smart. Stoic."

"Not your type?"

"Apparently." Her smile widens. "You really like him, huh?"

"It's casual."

"But you do?"

"I do."

"And you have been working together," she says. "It's not a lie."

Right. We've been working together for weeks. On a personal project. That's plenty of cause for blushing. "You think Simon will believe that?"

"I think you can play that *you don't get it because you're a guy* card."

"And when has Simon ever had a crush on an authority figure?"

"Have you actually asked?"

"Ew."

"Maybe there was a sexy math teacher."

"Why math?"

"A sexy English teacher."

"EWWW!"

She laughs. "Liam is right. You're too easy."

"Liam is right. You're as cruel as you are beautiful."

"Thank you?"

"I'm sure he means it as a compliment."

"Do you?"

I motion *eh*.

She laughs again. "Are you ready to face him?"

"Which him?"

"The room?"

No, but I can't hide in here forever. "As long as you'll back me up."

"Of course." She nods. "And my bra hook was broken. That's the emergency."

"Got it."

She takes a deep breath and marches back to the table.

I follow her with considerably less confidence.

Of course, only Liam pays Briar any attention. He flirts with his fiancée the way he normally does.

Simon and Max focus on me.

"All fixed," I say.

"Your Thai Iced Tea." Simon motions to the bright orange drink on the table. Well, the untouched one. He also has a Thai iced tea. "No dairy, all coconut. I checked."

"Thanks," I say.

"The food should be out soon," he says.

"Is that your excuse for an attitude today?" Liam asks Simon.

"What attitude?" Simon shrugs, effortless and unmoved.

For a split second, Liam frowns. The troublemaker can take any reaction except no reaction. But he's also a Pierce through and through. He doesn't give up easily. He turns his frown upside down.

I sit and smooth my jeans. "Don't mind Liam. He's difficult." Shit. They said they were friends. "Extra difficult around Simon."

"So I see." Max stays calm.

"How do you know Liam?" Simon asks.

"Work," Max says.

"Really?" Simon raises a brow. "I don't remember Pierce looking into Paytron."

"My life doesn't revolve around Pierce," Liam says, though it's not totally true. He's the CFO, and he's engaged to his former assistant. "It was for Bri. I was looking for a mentor for her. Someone who wouldn't bore her to death the way you would."

"You didn't tell me," Briar plays along.

"It's supposed to be a surprise," Liam says. "But Max here—"

"All artist, no business." Max draws a doodle in the air.

"I don't believe that," Simon says.

"I've learned over the years. But Raul was the one who knew business. My late partner," Max says.

Liam shoots Simon a *way to kill the mood* look.

Simon doesn't react.

"Is that how you came to teach Opal's class?" Simon asks.

Max nods. "I promised him I'd fill in if something happened. I'm sure it sounds ridiculous—"

"No, I understand," Simon says. "I made my late brother a promise and felt compelled to follow through, even though he…" He lets out a soft, sad laugh. "That's how I ended up with Vanessa, actually."

"Oh?" Max raises a brow. It's different than the way Simon does it. It's all Max.

"I shouldn't tell that story in front of Opal," Simon says.

"We can go." I motion to Briar. "We can take the food to Liam's place." And pretend this never happened, maybe.

"It is a bit hypocritical," Briar says. "If you'd tell the story in front of Liam or Adam. Unless… sorry, you don't want to hear it, do you?"

"Does it matter if I want to hear it?" I don't. Not usually. But Vanessa is the only topic that will actually distract Simon. "The three of you"—I point to Briar and Liam, then to Simon—"are sex-crazed perverts."

Briar smiles knowingly.

Liam too. "Oh yeah? I'm a sex crazed pervert? And you—"

"Liam, cede the floor for a minute, huh? We're talking about Simon's sex life," I say.

"Since when do you want to hear?" Simon asks.

"I love your love," I say.

"At least fill me in." Max keeps his voice the perfect mix of polite and interested. "Who is Vanessa?"

"His girlfriend," I say.

"Vanessa Moyer. She's an activist," Briar says.

"She runs a nonprofit." Simon's voice drips with pride. It's sweet. Or it would be, if I wasn't worried about keeping him on topic. Erm. Off topic.

Max stays focused. "How did you meet?"

"He's wanted to bone her since the first day of high school," Liam says.

Simon actually blushes. "She was the most beautiful woman I'd ever seen. She still is."

"But she was too smart to want anything to do with him," Liam says.

"We were rivals for a long time," Simon says.

"In competition?" Max asks.

Simon nods.

"That can be fun," Max says.

"It was," Simon says.

"And now they compete for dominance in bed?" Liam asks.

Briar clears her throat.

Liam shrugs *what?*

"Don't worry. I'm used to him," Simon says. "Sometimes, but I won't torture Opal with details."

"You're in love," Max says.

"Deeply," Simon says.

"It looks good on you," Max says.

"It does, doesn't it?" Briar asks.

Simon looks away, shy.

It's strange. Kind of cute. And kind of ick too. Those are way too many details.

Thankfully for him, the server spares him from the specific topic.

He drops off our plates and silverware. We shift into usual dinner talk. How is this dish? What is that dish? Everyone try Opal's too spicy for any sane person noodles (I do get them at a ten out of five, which costs an extra dollar).

Everyone tries, deems the noodles too hot for any sane person, keeps the conversation on food and work and Simon and Vanessa's relationship.

And Briar even answers a few questions about wedding planning (not really happening—despite the ring on her left hand, she's afraid of commitment) without grimacing.

Max is a good conversationalist. Quick, witty, generous.

He's perfect here too. With my family. As terrifying as it is.

For a solid hour, we talk. Then he leaves with Liam and Briar, and Simon and I head home, fix dessert and decaf coffee, talk about school.

He acts normal.

Like he believes Liam's story.

He even waits until I'm wishing him good night to strike.

Then he stands straight and looks me dead in the eyes and asks, "Are you sleeping with your professor?"

Chapter Eighteen

OPAL

Are you sleeping with your professor?

My hands never sweat, but all of a sudden, my palms are clammy. My jeans are too tight. My heart is pounding way too fast.

Was that really decaf coffee?

I'm wound tight in the worst possible way.

"What?" It's the only response I have.

"Are you sleeping with Max Morrison?" He repeats the question in a calm, even voice. As if he's asking me what I want to do this weekend.

"Why would you think that?"

"Your professor walked you to my office."

"He was meeting Liam."

"No, he wasn't."

"We're working on a project together," I say. "Outside of class."

"What kind of project?"

"An artist project. He's an artist."

"Where is his work?"

"I don't know," I say. "He uses a pen name. An artist name, I guess. I've only seen sketches." I want to see more. Everything. Everywhere. But I can't let my thoughts wander. I need to seem as neutral as Simon does. "I can ask if you want."

"Can I see?"

"When it's done."

"That's all it is?"

"Do you think I'm that—"

"I'm not blind."

"Okay, yes. I blush when he's around. I get nervous and flustered. I like him."

"You like him?"

"Yes, Simon. I know it's silly and stupid and immature, but I do. Thank you for forcing me to admit it."

"That's all? You like him?"

"I'm going to bed."

"I'll kill him if he hurts you."

"That's a very reasonable response."

"If he hurts you, it is."

"By not falling in love with me?"

"No."

"What if I want him to hurt me?" Fuck.

Fuck.

Fuck.

I try to pull the words back, but that's impossible. There's no rewind button here. The words spread around the room. They fill the space with the immense weight of my possible sexual preferences.

And my brother's knowledge of them.

Fuck.

Simon's voice drops to a tone that's all concern. "Is that what you're doing with him?"

"It's only—"

"Is that what you want?"

"Simon. Please."

"We can discuss this."

"We cannot discuss this."

"Yes." He places his palm on the kitchen island. "We can. We're both adults."

"You're my brother."

"I'm still your guardian."

"Please—"

"I know it's uncomfortable, but it's important. If there's anything you want to know, I'll find out."

"I don't want to know anything."

"Would you rather talk to Vanessa?"

"No."

"Briar?"

"Maybe."

"Have you?"

"A little."

"Can I talk to her? Make sure she's telling you what you need to know?"

"Can you end me now so I don't have to have this conversation?"

"No."

"I don't need your assistance. I have the Internet."

"The Internet isn't a good place to learn."

"Simon—"

He interrupts me with a laugh.

"I'm glad this amuses you."

"It's fair. After all those jokes about threesomes."

"They weren't jokes."

He raises a brow. "When was your last?"

"Last night."

"You were home all night."

"Whatever."

"Are you sleeping with Max?"

"Yes. We're having foursomes—"

"With the guys from art class who double-teamed you?" He uses my old joke against me.

"Shut up."

He smiles. "I won't press."

"Thank you."

"But you can trust me with this."

He is calmer now. More reasonable.

"I promise not to freak out. As long as you're being safe. Even if you are sleeping with your professor."

Not going there. "Even if I'm doing four guys at once?"

"No matter how many people you do at once."

"Okay… Thanks, I guess."

"You're welcome."

"I'm leaving now."

"I love you. No matter what."

"I love you too. But, Simon?"

"Yes?"

"Please don't make me talk about this again."

He shakes his head *no deal*, but I choose to ignore it. I lock myself in my room and wait for my embarrassment to dissipate.

It doesn't, but it lessens.

After two hours, I give up and look for a different distraction.

Max.

Opal: Did you escape Liam?

Max: He walked me home.

Opal: Of course.

Max: He cares about you.

Opal: He cares about making my life difficult.

Max: Yes. But he cares too. He was trying to get a pulse on me. Deem me worthy or not worthy of his little sister.

Opal: Liam? Really?

Max: Trust me. I'm an older brother.

Opal: And a younger brother.

Max: Even so.

Opal: You really think Liam is worried about whether or not you're worthy of me?

Max: I do.

How do I phrase this? I don't want him to think I'm obsessed with my family's approval. I don't want Max to think I expect anything from him, long term.

But I want to know what Liam said.

Does he see Max as worthy?

If, somehow, this became more than a fling—

It won't—

But if I did—

Opal: What do you think? Did you pass?

Max: I'm not sure. He's hard to read.

Opal: Was he polite? Or did he make stupid jokes?

Max: Stupid jokes.

Opal: That means he likes you.

Max: He must really like me.

Opal: Take it as a compliment.

Max: You're funny with your family. Nervous.

Opal: How would you be?

Max: Simon is the brother with the beige apartment?

Opal: Formerly beige apartment.

Max: Now?

Opal: Pink everywhere. And purple. His girlfriend's favorite color.

Max: He loves her.

Opal: He does.

Max: He's protective of you.

Opal: Over-protective.

Max: Don't blame him. He can't help it.

Opal: Because he's an older brother.

Max: Because you're sweet. It's a natural instinct to protect you.

That means something, but I don't press. I hold it close.

Max: I have to go. I'll see you tomorrow.

Opal: Good night, Max.

Max: Good night, Opal.

I think about him all night, dream about him, draw him, imagine him. I barely manage class, dinner, a barre class with Izzie.

Then I'm there, in his office Friday, ready for another lesson.

―――

Max is inspiring. As a teacher and a *teacher*. I'm drawing more than ever. And I'm more excited to show off my work.

Now that I have an outline for my project, I move quickly. I put the finishing touches on a project during our session. Plan the rest.

After, he bends me over his desk, pushes my jeans to my ankles, wraps his tie around my wrist, and he fucks me so hard I see stars.

All week, I'm in a daze of Max and art.

The next Friday is the same. Hours focused on my project, perfecting the work. This time, we go to his place. He strips me naked on the balcony, pushes me against the wall, fucks me right there.

The next week is the same. No, better. Hours of work. A long session in his apartment. Real bondage rope this time. He ties me to his bed, licks me until I come so many times I'm screaming, fucks me senseless.

I barely make it home.

My life is a perfect blur of school and art and Max and Izzie.

Then it's the week of our last session.

And Max asks a big question.

Max: Do you want something special this time?

I do. But the thing I really want seems more forbidden than anything.

I want a lot of dirty, illicit things from Max. But most of all?

I want him to kiss me.

A real, passionate, tender kiss on the lips.

Opal: What do you have in mind?

Max: Anything. Rougher. Softer. In public. With someone watching.

Opal: You'd agree to that?

Max: If it was what you wanted, I'd find a way.

Max Morrison, the perfect, tender, caring man… exclusively when it comes to my dirtiest desires.

Opal: I do want something.

Not the kiss; I can't ask for that.

But something else he won't want to offer—

Something I really, really want to try—

Opal: A role-play.

Max: Anything.

Opal: Student-teacher. Me as the student. You as the teacher. I want you to punish me.

He doesn't reply for a long time.

Max: Come early Friday. Wear pink.

Opal: Anything pink?

Max: Surprise me.

Chapter Nineteen

MAX

All week, my thoughts swirl.

The end of my time with Opal.

My need to protect her.

My desire to run from the pain in New York.

The fear of release—

Her.

Raul.

Grief.

It's not just the warmer weather—there are plenty of spring storms. It's not my increasing familiarity with the city, the office, the apartment.

It's something else.

Some burden he left on my shoulders.

Some burden I'm releasing.

This is it. My last promise to my best friend. My final chance to protect him.

When I finish my last lecture, I feel it lift. All at once, I'm a million pounds lighter.

I nearly float home.

Even with Opal, with every molecule in my body desperate

to claim her, I hold true to my promise to help her. We spend our last work session putting the finishing touches on her project.

We work through dinner (obscenely spicy Thai food). We work past our usual stopping time. We work until we're done.

"There." She stands and stretches her arms over her head. "Is that really it? Is it really done?"

"It is."

"That's… the end, isn't it?"

"The beginning," I say.

She doesn't argue. "I… I made something for you. For… later." She blushes and bends to pull something from her backpack. A set of drawings.

Two portraits. One of her. One of me.

Two halves of a whole.

Both perfect in their pop art collage.

Bold colors, thick lines, clear expressions.

The two of us, tied together, forever in her work.

It's perfect.

"Thank you." A million words rise in my throat. None are right. None are enough.

I don't want to say goodbye to her.

I don't want to let go of her.

I don't want to let go of Raul.

It's tangled. It's fucked up.

I care about her. I do. And I want the best for her. I want the world for her.

But that isn't enough.

"Opal—" I don't know what to say. How to explain it. How to leave her better than I found her, so she knows how much she means to me, so she's free to spread her wings.

"Don't tell me if you don't like it. I'd rather pretend."

"I love it."

"Then… let's leave it there, okay?" She blushes. "I'll imagine it hanging on your walls in California."

"In my bedroom," I say.

"You don't want people to see?"

"I want it to be mine."

"Will you… I know… will you send me a picture when you hang it? If you hang it? Please."

"Yes." I place the art on my desk and wrap my arms around her. "Thank you."

"It's nothing."

It's everything, but I don't say that. I still don't know what to say. Only what I owe her: one last lesson. "Can you spend the night?"

"Sure."

"I don't have the energy to do this properly."

"In the morning then?"

"In the morning."

She beams. It's too much. It's selfish, inviting her into my bed, but I do it anyway.

I help her pack her things; I walk her to my place; I make the space comfortable for her.

She showers, dresses in one of my spare t-shirts, settles into my bed.

She's perfect there.

And I want her there, forever.

But I can't have that.

I can only have this.

For the first time in a long time, my sleep is free. Easy. My morning is sweet.

We linger over breakfast and coffee, until she's wearing her eagerness on her face.

And then I begin.

"Go to the bedroom and wait," I say.

"For how long?"

"Until I decide you've waited long enough."

Chapter Twenty

MAX

Before my ex and I drifted apart, we tried to make it work. We were a good fit, intellectually. The same goals. Overlapping interests. Complementary strengths.

But here?

We never *really* fit.

She tried, but she liked what she liked.

No rope.

No orders.

Certainly no punishments.

At the time, I resented her lack of willingness to experiment. Now? Preparing to step into my bedroom and role-play a scenario with Opal? One that barely qualifies as role-play?

I didn't give Cassie enough credit.

My heart is thudding.

My breath is choppy.

My stomach?

The mix of nerves and need have me in free fall. I want to give this to her. That, I understand.

But the level of *my* desire?

It's terrifying.

How can I want to hurt this woman who trusts me?

Even if it's what she wants too.

I have experience here. I have wisdom. I'm here to teach her.

It's fucked up beyond belief. This entire situation is fucked up beyond belief.

But it's what we both want.

And, for the first time in a long time, I'm giving in to that.

I take a deep breath and release a steady exhale.

Bit by bit, breath by breath, I let go of my anxiety.

I step into my role.

I count to ten. Fifty. A hundred.

I slip into the room.

Opal is sitting on the black sheets, her legs pressed together, her hands on her knees, her attention on me.

She's wearing the same outfit—dark jeans and a hot pink blouse. The bedroom is arranged the same way—the bed against the wall, parallel to the mirror, perpendicular to the window.

But the air is different. The air is charged with the electric current running between us.

"Ms. Pierce." I push an exhale through my nose. "What are you doing here?"

"Waiting," she says.

She enjoys waiting. It winds her tighter. It does my job for me.

I should appreciate it, revel in making her wait, but I'm lacking patience. I'm always lacking patience with her.

Still.

I count to ten. Twenty. Thirty.

I give her the chance to steer the scene.

She doesn't.

She sits up straighter.

"Is there something you'd like?" I ask.

"Extra credit."

"I don't give out extra credit."

"Is that a policy?" Her eyes flit to mine. Her chest heaves with her inhale.

"A strict one."

"I can't convince you?" Her eyes travel down my body slowly. "I'm willing to do anything."

Fuck.

"I could be completely at your service."

"Completely?"

There's no hesitation in her voice. "Completely."

I need to match her. "Why should I consider you, Ms. Pierce?"

"I see the way you look at me." She stands. "Tell me you don't think about me." She pulls her blouse over her head and drops it on the floor. "Tell me you don't think about this."

"You have the wrong idea."

"Because you don't want me?"

"Because I don't cross the line."

"Never? Not even once?"

"Never."

She takes a half step toward me. "But you want to."

"No."

"No?" She reaches behind her back and undoes the hook of her bra. "I don't believe you."

This is it. The order she can disobey. The dare she can take. "Keep your clothes on."

She pushes the straps from her shoulders.

The nylon fabric falls on top of her blouse.

And there she is, Opal Pierce, in only her jeans in my bedroom.

So similar to where we've been.

But so far too.

"Don't defy me." I don't have the force I need in my voice.

But she takes it anyway. "Or?"

"Or I'll punish you."

"Then punish me." She undoes the button of her jeans and takes another step toward me.

I seize the opportunity. I meet her, hook my arm around her hip, push her onto the bed.

It's hard enough she bounces.

A gasp catches in her throat. She looks up at me, thrilled and certain and completely committed to this.

Fuck.

She's perfect.

She deserves better.

She deserves everything.

I'm here, and I'm giving her what I can.

It's not enough.

But it's what I have.

I move quickly. I follow her onto the bed. Grab her by the belt loops. Pull her down the bed.

Then up, so she's next to me.

I straighten and pull Opal over my lap, her forehead on the sheets, her stomach on my thighs, her ass in the air.

"You think you can tease me?" I place my hand low on her back. Softly, to start. A warning.

"Yes."

"You think you can tempt me?"

"Yes."

"Bad girl."

She turns her head.

"I will punish you." I press her a little harder, so she can feel my cock, hard against her stomach.

A groan falls from her lips. "Max—"

"Professor Morrison—"

"Please."

"Please, what?"

"I only want you."

"You want to defy me."

"No. I want to please you. However I can."

"Bad girl," I say it again.

A murmur of approval falls from her lips.

I keep one hand on her lower back. I hold her in place as I push her jeans off her hips.

Then the perfect pink panties.

Opal Pierce, bent over my knee, awaiting my punishment.

What the fuck happened to my life?

I push aside the absurdity. The fucked-up nature of our relationship. The expiration date.

I push aside everything except my desire to hurt her.

And please her.

And command her.

Everything she wants.

Everything I want.

"You want me to fuck you?" I press my palm into her back.

She reaches for something. Gets the sheets. "Yes."

"You think you can play with me?"

"Yes."

"No." I raise my hand and bring it down on her ass. It's hard enough to hurt, but barely.

"Yes."

"No." I do it again. A little harder. "I make the rules."

"Max—"

"Professor Morrison." My voice drops an octave.

"Professor—"

"You don't tempt me." I bring my hand down on her ass again. Hard. Hard enough to hurt.

"Fuck."

"I tempt you." Again. "I tease you." Again. "I play with you." Again.

Her breath hitches in her throat. "Professor—"

Again. "Yes?"

"Please."

Again. "Please."
"Please. Fuck me."
"No."
"Please."

I bring my hand on her ass hard. "Not until you learn respect."

She groans as I spank her again.

Again.

Again.

Harder.

Hard enough, she gasps.

Then yelps.

Hard enough to push her.

Again.

Again.

"Fuck." She tugs at the sheets.

She's at the brink of what she can take.

But, still, I bring my hand on her flesh again.

Again.

Again.

I raise my hand.

But this time, I bring it to her cunt.

No tease. No warning.

I slip two fingers inside her and push deep.

She groans as she takes me.

She's wet and ready, but still, I stretch her.

"Fuck. Ma—Professor."

The last bit of blood flees my brain. I need to be inside her, now. But I need to do this first.

I need every fucking thing I can have with her.

I drive my fingers into her with steady strokes.

She turns her head, squirming against my thighs as I work her.

Again and again—

Until I'm sure I've pushed her far enough.

Then I bring my thumb to her clit. A few strokes, and she's there, pulsing against my fingers, groaning my name as she comes.

I work her through her orgasm, then I push her onto the bed, on her stomach.

I pull her to the edge, spread her legs, hold her in place as I undo my belt and unzip my slacks.

I take one moment to savor the perfect sight.

Then I drive into her.

Fuck.

My eyes close.

My fingers dig into her hips.

She's warm, wet, perfect.

Mine.

For the last time, she's mine.

I pull back, push her up the bed, climb on with her.

Then I push her knees apart, lower my body onto hers, push into her.

She gasps as I pull back and drive into her again.

This is as close as we'll ever be.

The last fucking time.

I wrap my hand around her throat.

I bury my face in her neck.

And I fuck her with hard, deep thrusts.

She's there fast, groaning my name as she pulses around me.

It pulls me over the edge.

My eyes close. My fingers dig into her hip.

I pull her closer.

I run my teeth along her shoulder, marking her for the last time.

Claiming her, for the last time.

One with her, for the last time.

Fuck.

Pleasure rocks through me. Waves so deep and intense, I almost lose my balance.

I work through my orgasm, then I collapse next to her.

This time, I don't right my clothes.

I slide over and do away with every layer, and I lie next to Opal until her breath is normal.

Until she's calm and safe and settled into reality.

Then for a while longer.

"Good?" I brush a long, dark strand behind her ear.

"Great." She presses her lips into a smile. "Thank you, Max." She looks up at me through hooded eyes. "I, uh, I should get dressed. I have to meet my brother."

"Do you need help?"

"No. I'm good. I just… I wanted to ask you one thing."

"Yeah?"

She slides out of the bed and pulls my cotton robe over her shoulders. "Will you kiss me?"

Chapter Twenty-One

OPAL

Will you kiss me?

My stomach flutters. My fingers curl into my palms.

It's absurd. All that and I'm nervous about a kiss. But I am.

A kiss is intimate in a different way. A kiss is dripping with love and affection.

"It's okay if you want to say no." My cheeks flush. "It won't hurt my feelings."

"It won't?"

Of course it will, but I don't want to push him too hard. I already pushed him here. "A little."

He stands and looks me in the eyes.

It's wild. He's naked—completely and totally naked—but I can't look away from his dark eyes. There's so much in them. Need and desire and affection.

"I have something for you first."

"Another round?"

"No." He laughs. "A gift." He closes the space between us. "You should get dressed."

"I know."

"You have to go."

"I know."

He runs his fingers over the robe. "I'll miss you, Opal."

"I'll miss you too."

"If you need advice. About art. Or partners—"

"Okay."

"Promise you'll call?"

"Text."

His smile is sad.

"I promise."

"Thank you." He leans closer, but he doesn't kiss me on the lips. Not yet. He presses his lips to my jaw. My neck. My shoulder. "I'll meet you in the main room. Give me two minutes."

"Okay."

He steps into the bathroom and closes the door.

I ignore the knot in my stomach. I don't want to say goodbye. I can't say goodbye. But what else can I do?

I dress. I gather my things. I pace around the kitchen.

Max emerges from the bedroom in only jeans—

He owns jeans—

No shirt, no shoes—

With something in his arms.

A small black sketchbook wrapped in a hot pink bow.

"This is for you." He meets me in the middle of the room. "But do me a favor?"

"Anything."

"Don't look in front of me."

Is he really embarrassed? That's hard to imagine. And I want to see his face when I open this. I want to see every bit of his reaction.

But I asked for something I want—

This is only fair.

"Sure." I slip the sketchbook into my backpack. "Thank you."

"It's been…"

"Fun?"

"Meaningful." He slips his arm around my waist.

He leans closer. For a second, his eyes catch mine. Then his lids flutter closed and his lips find my lips.

He kisses me softly.

Then harder.

My lips part. His tongue swirls around mine, dancing with mine, claiming mine.

Only that's not right.

Not anymore.

But right now, for one more perfect moment, he's mine, and we're locked together.

Max kisses me with everything he has, then he pulls back and brushes my hair behind my ear. "Take care, Opal."

"Take care." It's not *I love you*, but it's something all the same. I swallow the other words that rise into my throat, I lift my backpack, and I leave.

This time, he doesn't insist on walking me out.

And I don't ask.

I take the subway home. I sit through lunch with my brother. I even spend the afternoon with Izzie, talking through another potential makeup with Jaime.

I hold it together until I'm alone in my room.

Until I look at the sketchbook.

Max's work. Pages and pages of self-portraits. Images of the city. Drawings of me.

And in the corner of every one, his signature.

The name he uses for his work.

He isn't mine anymore.

But this is.

And this is forever.

It will feel good one day, but right now—

I climb under the covers, I hug my sketchbook, and I cry.

Chapter Twenty-Two

MAX

My condo is a strange place. In every external way, it's the same space. The wide windows still let in the white morning light and the blistering afternoon sun. The hardwood floors still squeak. The counters still shine.

And my bed, the just-firm-enough foam memory mattress, still invites me. I settle into my cotton sheets late. Wake early.

Still on East Coast time.

Still unsettled.

This isn't home. But it is home too.

It's the space Cassie and I shared.

The space where I started this business with Raul.

Where I lost him.

Where I lost the sense of safety and home.

One thing is the same, I need coffee this early. I fix a dark roast in my French Press. Drink it black. Think of Opal's reaction.

Would she accept the explanation? There isn't fresh food here yet. No milk of any kind.

But I could have picked it up on the way home. Or asked Cassie to grab something for me. She still has a key.

But who asks their ex-girlfriend to grab almond milk?

After I finish my cup, I dress, take a walk along the path overlooking the beach.

The soft white light fades into a bright blue sky. Waves roll onto the sand. Tourists circle streets, looking for free parking.

It's late May. Early in the season. Most people are locals. Well, Orange County locals. They're coming from Tustin or Irvine or Santa Ana.

But I can already feel the shift in energy. The bikini-clad women and men in board shorts. Beach volleyball and soft boards.

The beach is beautiful and it's perfect. In every state. In every season.

There's nowhere like it.

Not even the engineering marvel of New York City.

Even if everything else was different, that would be there.

Opal belongs in the city.

I don't.

I watch the waves roll into the beach until a text grabs my attention.

Cassie.

Cassie: I hear you got home last night.

Max: I did.

Cassie: Re-christen the bed yet?

Max: How else would I deal with jet lag?

Cassie: A walk on the beach?

Max: Guilty.

Cassie: In all black? You're a New Yorker now.

Max: Because I never wore black before.

Cassie: Are you?

Max: No. I'm in California mode.

Cassie: There's a mode?

Max: Apparently.

Cassie: A neon orange speedo?

Max: So you still have sexual fantasies of me?
Cassie: Honestly?
Max: Don't break my heart.
Cassie: No. I don't. But I appreciate an attractive man.
Max: Brutal.
Cassie: Will you be home in ten?
Max: Don't you have a key?
Cassie: It's officially your place now. I ask permission.

She moved out while I was in New York.

Max: Anytime is fine. What do you need?
Cassie: A few things. I'll bring coffee.
Max: I had coffee.
Cassie: And you don't want more?
Max: Fair.
Cassie: Still drink it black?
Max: Almond milk now.
Cassie: You went to New York to fall behind the trends?
Max: How am I behind the trends?
Cassie: Oat milk is the new thing.
Max: Was the new thing last year.
Cassie: Okay. Dark roast. Almond milk. See you soon.

I slip my phone into my pocket. Take a deep breath. Find no resistance.

My shoulders don't tense. My chest doesn't tighten.

It's easy talking to Cassie now.

Even with how things ended.

Even with the months before that.

Is it the impersonal nature of texts? Or something deeper?

The thought circles my mind as I walk home, shower, dress in jeans and a fresh t-shirt. I barely recognize my reflection. Who is this version of Max? The casual man who isn't hiding behind designer gear?

I haven't seen him in a long, long time.

Cassie either. She knocks, lets herself in, finds me in the

bedroom. "Like Narcissus before him, Max Morrison was paralyzed by his own beauty."

"As long as we agree I'm beautiful."

She meets my gaze through the mirror and raises a brow. "This is familiar, isn't it?"

"In a way."

She raises the takeout cup in her right hand. "Did you eat?"

"No."

"I brought sandwiches," she says. "Egg and cheese."

"Avocado?"

"It goes without saying."

I turn to face her.

She smiles, warm, familiar, uncertain. "Hey. You okay?"

"No."

"I figured." She hands me the coffee and leads me into the main room. The kitchen slash dining room slash den. A perfect mix of modern and cozy.

Once upon a time, it was the perfect mix of her and me. Now? I'm not sure. The touches of her are gone, but the space isn't me either.

Whoever that is.

"You look good," she says. "Tired, but handsome."

"Brutal again."

She puts the sandwiches on plates. Brings both to the table. "You cleaned the bed well. After your tryst."

"Of course." I sit. Pick up half my sandwich. "I'm an expert."

"Was there someone?"

"Last night?"

"No. Before." Her voice softens. "Before you left."

"Cassie—"

"I would understand. We hadn't been together in a long time."

"No. Never. Did you…"

"No."

The sandwich is perfect. Crisp bread, warm egg, soft, creamy avocado. "Thank you."

"For not cheating?"

"For breakfast. And not cheating."

"You're welcome. For breakfast. The other... I don't think it merits thanks." She takes a long sip of her coffee. "Was there someone in New York?"

"For a while."

"Now?"

"It was a fling."

"Some moody New Yorker who only wears black?"

"Is this your one impression of New York?"

"Who talks about the quality of the pizza."

"And bagels."

"And coffee." She smiles. "And spends every day roaming the MoMA."

"What do you have against the MoMA?"

"She does." She laughs.

"In pink."

"MoMA Barbie."

"Exactly."

She laughs. "Your type." She motions to her less than ample chest.

"Don't."

"Don't what?"

"Suggest I wasn't a fan of your body."

"MoMA Barbie isn't all tits and ass?"

"No. She's tall and slim."

"You just had to throw in tall, didn't you?" She shakes her head. "That's low."

"Like the shelves you can reach."

She flips me off.

I try the coffee. It's perfect too. And better with the almond milk. Softer. "Do you really want to discuss my sex life?"

"Yes."

That's strange.

Cassie folds her hands. "I wanted to apologize. For how I acted about your preferences."

"I pushed too hard."

"Yes, but I pushed back too hard. I realized something when I rebounded."

I raise a brow.

"I won't overdo the details."

"You can. I don't mind."

"You don't?"

No. There's no jealousy in my stomach. No desire to claim Cassie. I don't feel the pain of our distance anymore, but I feel it. We're worlds apart. I loved her. A part of me will always love her. But she's not mine and I'm not hers and that's okay. "I don't."

"We have that in common."

"You want to hear about my sex life?"

"No. Well, yes, I wouldn't mind. But I meant your tastes. We… have the same tastes."

"Oh."

"It surprised me too." Her cheeks flush. "And the tiger woman implications… But I do. I like being in control."

"You've tried?"

"A lot."

"You're safe?"

"Max."

"You showed up here to check on me."

She doesn't protest.

"I can check on you."

"I'm an adult. I don't need to be reminded to use protection. And I've been a woman my entire life. I've been careful around men since before you realized men were dangerous."

I deserve that.

"But, yes, I'm safe. One guy. Someone I know. Someone who confessed his interests a few years ago."

"Chad?"

Her blush deepens.

"He's actually named Chad?"

"He didn't pick it."

"Still."

"Don't be an asshole."

"I can't help it."

She nods in agreement.

"How is Chad?"

"Chad is the perfect sub." Her blush spreads to her chest. "I still feel strange saying it."

"You'll get used to it."

"You promise?"

I nod. "Will I find a leather corset in your closet?"

"And thigh-high boots."

"Really?"

"Maybe. Maybe not." She smiles and takes a bite of her sandwich. "I'm sure you'd like to know."

"I would."

She shrugs *too bad*, but she's not quite casual.

"He was tall."

"See? It hurts, doesn't it?"

"I'm tall enough," I say.

"He's taller."

I laugh. This is strange but normal, and all the stranger for how normal it feels. "Tall guys can't be submissive?"

"No. He's just… imposing. I'm surprised."

"And your new playmate?"

"She's not mine," I say.

"Was she sweet and innocent?"

"In some ways."

"All the pink?"

"And young."

She raises a brow *really?* "How young?"

"Too young."

"A barely legal thin New Yorker who wears only pink."

"Her main qualities, yes."

"As long as we're on the same page." She laughs and takes a long sip. "Do you miss her?"

"I do."

"Are you going to see her again?"

"I don't know. It was a fling."

"You should. I…" She takes a deep breath. "I'm worried about you, as a friend."

"Cassie—"

"Let me say this."

I nod.

She continues. "I know things were strained when we ended, but I meant what I said about wanting to be there for you. I can't imagine losing my best friend. And that way too… Are you dealing with it?"

"Here and there."

"Therapy?"

"You're recommending therapy?"

"I'm enlightened."

"Did Chad talk you into it?"

"Fuck off." She laughs. "He's sweet."

"I imagine."

"Seriously, Max. You know it's not your fault, right?"

I say nothing.

"Max."

"I don't know."

"Do you really think your best friend's suicide was about you?"

"I don't mean that."

"But you're guilty?"

"I ignored the signs. I believed he was the happy one. I was sure I was the one who'd end with that fate."

"Do you still?"

"I don't know."

"And your pink-loving girlfriend?"

"What about her?"

"Did she know him?" she asks.

"She did."

"What did she think?"

"She didn't see it either."

She raises a brow *see*.

"They weren't close."

"You weren't close either. Not anymore."

"But that—"

"Wasn't your fault either."

Maybe.

"It happens to everyone. We grow up, grow apart, want different things."

"We ran a business together."

She nods *true*. "But he wouldn't want this. He wouldn't want you to be miserable."

"It's early in the day for this level of attack?"

"It's noon in New York." She takes another bite of her sandwich. "What would Raul want?"

"To hear about you and Chad."

She laughs. "For you?"

"For me to hear about you and Chad."

"Then…"

"He'd want to hear about my—"

"Playmate?"

"Opal."

"Like the rock?"

I nod.

"And you made fun of Chad?"

"Opal is better than Chad."

She motions *sorta*. "How is Opal?"

"I don't know. Hurt, probably."

"She didn't want it to end?"

"I was her first."

"You slept with a virgin?"

"Her first… playmate."

"Is that all it is?" she asks.

"I don't know."

"Do you love her?"

"I might."

Her cheeks curl into a smile. "I can't believe it."

"Because I'm not capable?"

"No… how normal this feels. How happy I am, for you. Really, Max. You deserve good things."

I swallow hard.

"Even if you did fail Raul—which you didn't. But even if you did. You deserve to be happy. And it's what he'd want."

"It doesn't make sense."

"Because she's a pink-loving New Yorker?"

"For a lot of reasons."

"Did you like New York?"

"Things about it."

"Are you thinking of defecting?"

"No."

"East Coast, least coast."

"West Coast, best coast," I agree.

"Opal… go fuck her again?"

"Doesn't rhyme."

"Shit. I better work on that." She smiles. "You miss her a lot."

"And?"

"And? I'm the pragmatic one. If you love her—"

"I didn't say that."

"If you love her and you miss her, why not go for it?"

"Details are important."
"But is there anything you can't overcome?"
No. Maybe. I don't know anymore.
"Go for it. For Raul."
"You're playing that card again?"
"Absolutely."
"It's bullshit."
"It's what he'd want though."
It is.

After Cassie leaves, I do what I always do when I can't clear my head. I draw.

For hours, I sketch. Abstract shapes. Images of New York skyscrapers, California coastlines, beautiful women in knee-high boots or sandals.

Opal, in a million positions, with a thousand expressions.

Exactly where I want her.

It's obvious.

She's what I want.

I need to go to her. To find her. To talk to her.

I book a flight for first thing tomorrow. Try to find the words, to figure out exactly what I want to say.

But I'm too slow.

She's here.

Chapter Twenty-Three

OPAL

"Hey." I don't know what else to say. I don't know how else to start. "You look good."

"Tired?"

"Handsome." I want to touch him, to reach over and feel the soft fabric of his shirt, the rough denim of his jeans, but I keep my hands at my sides. "Really handsome. I… I've never seen you in a t-shirt. It suits you."

"More than a tie?"

"I don't know. I like both. I, uh…"

"Do you want to come in?"

"Yes. Thank you."

He pulls the door open for me.

I step inside. Take in the wide, open space. So different than Max's sparse apartment in the city, but so similar too. The same wide windows and sleek furniture. The same coffee maker on the counter. The same black frames.

But all these touches of him.

A blanket draped over the couch. A pop art book on the coffee table. A shelf overflowing with books. Framed prints hung on the walls. An eclectic mix. Wood-block prints, impressionist paintings, cubist, pop art.

It's not his style as an artist—his lines are simple and minimalist, the opposite of mine—but it suits him just the same. It's really his home. His place.

"Do you want something to drink?" he asks.

"It's barely afternoon."

"Coffee?"

"I shouldn't. I had a lot on the plane. And I… I'm already nervous." I wipe my palms on my sundress.

"You look good."

"Not too pink?"

"On you? Never."

My heart thuds against my chest. "Maybe water."

"You're declining coffee?"

"I am."

"It's that serious?"

"It is."

He nods with understanding, fills two glasses, brings one to me.

"The semester is over."

"It is."

"And I know… you're back here. And you don't have plans to leave."

"I don't."

"But I… I don't have summer plans. And I don't have to be in New York until the end of August. I'm not saying I'd stay here—I have an Air BnB. With my friend Izzie. Well, eventually. She wants to see how she likes California, but her boyfriend is up in Malibu, and we're not really near Malibu, are we? But she knows how to drive and she isn't even sure if she wants to get back together with him, so—"

"Opal—"

"Yes—"

"Stay."

"Are you sure?"

"I am." He closes the space between us. "Stay. For as long as you want."

"All summer?"

"All summer."

"And after?"

"I don't know." He brings his hand to my cheek. Runs his thumb over my temple. "But I know it will be a hell of a summer." He leans down and presses his lips to mine.

He kisses me like he's claiming me.

Maybe it's not forever.

But it's for now.

And, right now, that's everything.

Epilogue

OPAL

"Is it like this everyday?" Izzie raises her sunglasses for a better view of a tall man in a small swimsuit.

"You're staying four blocks away."

"All by myself."

"I visit."

"Not enough."

"If you want me there, say the word."

"No. You look so needy when you sleep over. Like you just can't handle another night without Max's hand around your throat."

My cheeks flush.

Izzie smiles, victorious. She loves to make me uncomfortable. And though I'm more comfortable with my desires these days… I'm not comfortable talking about them with her.

She holds her hand over her eyes, deems the gesture insufficient, returns the shades to their previous position. "It's bright here."

"Oddly bright."

"You fit in though." She motions to my hot pink bikini top, my bare feet, my wavy-from-the-salt-water hair. Then to her own still blue (but faded from the sun and salt) locks, her red heart-shaped sunglasses, her black bikini, her black fingernail polish, the brand spankin' new tattoo on her hip (a bright blue butterfly).

"Me…"

"I do not."

"You do too, Opes. You're a total Malibu Barbie."

"We're not in Malibu."

"Newport Beach Barbie."

"I'm too flat to be a Barbie."

She laughs. "True."

"Hey!"

"Real friends are honest."

"And you fit perfectly in Venice Beach."

She motions *sorta*.

"No. You're right. You were too hip for every place in the even-hipper-than-St. Mark's-used-to-be street. The one with that coffee shop with six-dollar drinks."

"I was."

"And this—" I motion to her new tattoo. A 'sign of her freedom' after her official break-up with Jamie. And 'sure to piss off her mom.' Though I'm not sure when her mom is going to see it, given the location.

It is cool. And extremely sexy. And exactly Izzie.

And the tattoo artist who adorned her skin—

He was smoking hot, super cool, and extremely enamored with her. He left his card, but she still hasn't called. At least, not as far as I know.

But then she's turning her "I need to irritate" energy on Max and me, claiming an interest in his younger brother, so she probably wouldn't tell me even if she had him locked in her bedroom.

Which…

Nothing would surprise me at this point.

"You fit into the tattoo shop perfectly," I say.

"You think I can get a job there?"

"Doing what?"

"Staring at hot guys?"

"Sounds like a nice gig."

"What do you think it pays?"

"Negative twenty dollars an hour?"

"I pay to do hard work?" she asks.

"Well, maybe if you do some *hard* work."

She laughs. "Hey! I don't do that kind of work for money."

"But you might tell your mom you do."

"Oh yeah, if she asks, you're very concerned about my choices." She takes a long sip of her iced latte. After an early afternoon of swimming, we left Max and his younger brother to their love of the ocean, went for coffee, returned to ogle.

The view is good here. Better than at our usual spot. Max lives in Corona Del Mar, a cozy neighborhood in Newport Beach, south of our current spot in Newport Beach proper.

The beach closest to his place, the one we walk most days, doesn't allow surfboards. Safer for kids. Packed with kids on the weekends. Screaming kids.

It's kind of alarming. Even with my history of diving into public pools during sweltering New York summers. I guess I'm too used to the Park Avenue lifestyle, because all the screaming—

It's not what I expect.

It's a lot, sometimes, but it's nice too. The excitement. The raw enthusiasm. The families.

Not that I think about a family with Max. I mean, not anytime soon. I'm happy with where I am. I'm happy to spend the summer swimming in possibilities.

But maybe one day…

I don't know.

I'm an artist. I have an active imagination. I envision all sorts of future possibilities. An exhibit in the MoMA. A vacation in the Caribbean. An adorable kid with dark hair and blue eyes. Which is probably not even possible, since Max's dad has dark eyes too, but uh—

"Are you seriously imagining your boyfriend naked right now?" Izzie asks.

"He's in a swimsuit."

"Ben too." She makes a show of staring. Not that we can see anything. The brothers are sitting atop surfboards way out in the distance.

This beach is packed with surfers and people watching surfers. It's the go-to spot. Something about waves hitting a jetty. (I'm not that California. Not yet anyway).

Though I have to admit… I like watching the surfers. There are so many different kinds of people, and they're all exactly where they're supposed to be. Men, women, old, young, blond, brunette, redhead. Even a few girls and guys with unusually colored hair. Which Izzie loves and hates in equal measure.

She gives up on ogling Ben and turns to me. "Are you still picturing his dick?"

"I was not picturing his dick."

"What were you picturing?"

"Romantic things."

"A wedding on the beach?"

"Shut up."

"You were?"

"I was not."

"That's adorable, Opes. Really."

My blush deepens.

"Aww… what sweet embarrassment."

"Don't say anything."

She mimes zipping her lips.

Can we discuss something else? Anything else. "How's your mom?"

"Happy! She's glad I'm in California all summer." She makes an *ugh* noise.

"She wants the place to herself," I say.

"Probably. She's probably having an affair with… what's her equivalent of a pool boy?"

"Doesn't your family have a house in the Hamptons?"

"Your family has *the* house in the Hamptons. It's not even a house. It's a freakin' castle."

"It's not the Hamptons." Technically. "And that's not my point."

"You think it is the pool boy?" she asks.

"Maybe."

"A pool boy… mister. Why isn't there a word for a male mistress?"

That is an injustice. "Do you really think your mom is cheating?"

"No. She's too square."

"And you'd actually admire the rebellion?"

"No." She slurps the last sip of her coffee. "A little. Are you coming over tonight?"

"Ben is leaving after dinner."

"So you and Max finally have the place to yourself again?"

"Ahem."

"Say no more. I'm not a c-blocker."

"Tomorrow," I say. "We'll spend the day together. Find a hip coffee shop. With all sorts of hot guys and girls with unusually colored hair. Or do you need to be the cool one?"

"You know I like squares like you, Opes."

"Rude."

"Real friends—"

"Are full of shit?"

"Sometimes."

"How about a real California girl?" I ask.

"With blond hair and fake tits?"

"No, the natural type. With great flexibility from yoga."

"She sounds too zen."

"A surfer boy?"

"Him too… but then Max isn't remotely zen and—" She looks to the beach as an extremely handsome man emerges from the surf. "Speak of the devil."

Max steps onto the sand, easy, confident, sexy as fuck. He holds his surfboard with one hand, runs his fingers through his hair with the other.

His dark locks are longer now, almost long enough to fall over his eyes. He's a different person in California. Easier. Freer. Constantly wearing very tight jeans that show off his amazing butt.

Not that my ability to stare at his ass is the important part of this. But, fuck, that tiny swimsuit—

His muscular thighs—

How is he so sexy in anything and everything?

"Oh my god. There's no way you're coming over tonight." Izzie laughs. "Good thing you're wearing a bikini, huh? Bet those bottoms are drenched."

"Don't be gross."

"No deal." She laughs as Max comes closer. She's laughing at me, at my inability to tear my eyes from his body, but I don't care.

He's perfect.

He's mine.

For this summer. And, maybe, for longer too.

"Max." Izzie nods hello.

"Izzie." He flashes her a dazzling smile. "Enjoying the view?"

"It's not bad." She turns toward something. "Getting better."

My lips curl into a smile. Max's smile… it's perfect. It's everything.

Somehow, I manage to follow her gaze. Of course, she's ogling Max's younger brother Ben.

I can't blame her. Ben is handsome. He looks a lot like Max, so, of course, he's handsome. He's probably more traditionally handsome, with his chiseled jaw and his broad shoulders. Where Max has intensity, Ben has lightness. Easiness. Like Liam, only significantly less annoying. Mostly.

"Are you trying to steal my baby brother's innocence?" Max deadpans.

"Absolutely," she returns.

Ben catches up. Shoots Izzie his own dazzling smile. "Isabel."

"Mr. Morrison." She smiles.

"Will you stay in California if you fall in love with him?" Max asks.

"Love? Who's talking about love?" Izzie teases.

"You need to be careful with Ben. He's a heartbreaker," Max says.

Ben nods *it's true*.

"My mom would hate it," she says.

"Good reason to do anything," Max says.

"You sound like your girlfriend," Izzie says.

We're not boyfriend girlfriend, exactly. We're not anything, except having fun for the summer, but he doesn't correct her. He just says, "She's a smart woman."

"And great taste too, right?" Ben teases him.

"I was going to say…" Max smiles.

My heart thuds against my chest.

His joy is effervescent. I need more. I need it all.

Even though I've had a lot. He still thinks about Raul, sometimes. He still falls into grief sometimes. But the rest of the time—

Well, a lot of the time, when he's with me—

He's not a happy-go-lucky guy, but he loves and laughs as intensely as he grieves.

Fuck, how did I get so cheesy?

I guess love does that to you.

He has a deep reserve of joy. Not the joy I see in other

people. Something sharper and harder to see and all the more beautiful because I'm the only one who sees it.

When we walk along the beach, or cook dinner together, or lie on the couch and draw, he's happy. We're happy.

It's not real life, exactly. I know. We're still in an in-between state. He only works a few days a week. I spend my free time on my art. We have this summer together, and it's all time and joy and light.

I don't know if I'll stay in California forever. But I know I'll be in New York soon. I have school. And he has a life here. It's complicated. Or it will be, come September.

But right now?

Right now, it's perfect.

"Is she drooling?" Ben asks.

"She's definitely drooling," Izzie says.

"I am not." I wipe my lip. Just in case. Absolutely no drool. But who could blame me for drooling over Max?

It's not his lean torso or his sculpted shoulders or his intense eyes—

Though I do appreciate the aesthetic appeal of those traits—

It's him. Some quality uniquely his.

"Put the girl out of her misery," Ben says.

"She enjoys the misery," Max says.

Izzie laughs and nods *true*.

Ben raises a brow.

"Stop laughing about my sex life." I can't muster any outrage. This is easy too. My best friend, my not-boyfriend, his brother, the sun, the surf.

Fuck, I'm listing the surf in my favorite things.

I love the beach. I tried to deny it for a long time, especially when I first visited the Pierce manor (it's on a windswept cliff, straight out of a Gothic romance novel), but I do. I love the salty breeze, the soft sand, the roar of the ocean.

And, of course, the sight of Max in a teeny, tiny swimsuit.

Okay, maybe I'm a little… obvious in my stare. A little.

"I can walk Isabel home," Ben says. "Leave you to it."

"Over my dead body," Max says, already protective of my best friend.

Izzie growls. "You don't trust your own brother?"

"I know my own brother," Max says.

Ben laughs.

"What did I tell you? He's a lot like Liam," Max says.

"Who is this dashing Liam I hear so much about?" Ben asks.

"He's dashing?" I ask.

"If he's a lot like me," Ben says.

Izzie laughs. "He's cute. And you have the same charming smile. What do you look like in a suit?"

"Irresistible," he says.

"He does wear a suit," Max agrees.

"I look good in everything," Ben says.

"Or nothing," Izzie suggests.

"We'll drop you off," Max says.

"No. It's only ten blocks. I want to walk. On my own." She blows Ben a kiss. "I'll miss you. Visit."

"Here? Or New York?"

"Both." Even though he's sopping wet, and she's in her denim shorts, she throws her arms around him. "But especially here. I won't be a free agent for long."

"Good things don't last," he says.

She laughs and releases him. "I'll see you tomorrow, Opes." She gives me a wet hug. Then gives Max one. "Put the girl out of her misery, huh?"

"Maybe," he says.

"He's cruel," Izzie says. "That must be why you like him."

I flip her off. She blows me a kiss. Then she turns and she practically skips to the sidewalk.

"Don't fuck her," Max says.

Ben just laughs. "I won't be long."

"Hey. If you're going to fuck her, make it count," I say.

Again, he laughs. "I'll be back next weekend. But only for dinner this time. I found a place in Venice."

"Izzie loves Venice," I say.

He smiles *I know*. "Ms. Pierce." He offers his hand. "I'm always honored to see you."

I shake. "You too."

He pulls me into a tight hug. Whispers in my ear. "Take care of him, okay?"

"Of course."

He releases me, hugs Max, whispers his own goodbye.

Max laughs. "You're incorrigible."

"My best quality." Ben winks at his brother. Then at me.

And then we're alone.

"Are they right?" Max asks. "Are you in misery?"

I nod.

"And you think I'm going to release you?"

I shake my head.

"You're a smart woman. That's one of the things I love about you."

"Does it mean you'll go easy on me?"

"I'll give you one guess."

Want More?

Get to know Opal's protective older brother Simon with *Ruthless Rival*, a sexy enemies with benefits romance. Turn the page for a sample.

Prefer to start with book one? Check out *Broken Beast*, a smoking hot *Beauty and the Beast* story.

All caught up on the Pierce Family? Get your sexy billionaire fix with *Dirty Deal*, a super steamy Cinderella story.

Ruthless Rival - Excerpt

VANESSA

Get Ruthless Rival Now

Most days, I'm good at resisting temptation.

But tonight?

Tonight, my gaze keeps flitting to the one man I shouldn't want: Simon Pierce.

The most powerful man in Manhattan.

The sexiest man in any room.

The man I've wanted and hated since the ninth grade.

Between handshakes and small talk, I watch his deep blue eyes scan the room. I study his soft lips. I imagine his strong hands on my skin.

For two hours, I mingle.

For two hours, I ignore the dirty thoughts circling my mind.

Finally, after my last *thanks for considering a donation* handshake, I slip out of the hotel ballroom, find the bar, order an Aviation.

One drink to celebrate the victories of the day.

Only I'm not drinking alone.

He's here.

"On me." Simon drops his credit card on the bar.

I swallow the *fuck off* that rises in my throat. The *fuck me* too. "Thanks." I'm well-mannered.

The same as him.

No, that's another way he bests me.

Since the first day of high school, Simon and I have competed.

Top grades?

Simon wins.

Better manners at a bar?

Simon wins.

Intense, panty-melting, desire-inspiring stare?

Simon definitely wins.

"My pleasure." He half-smiles. The Simon Pierce signature. Amused, above it all, hot as hell.

"For you?" the bartender asks.

"Whiskey, neat," he says.

"Coming right up," the bartender says.

"Whiskey, really? Are you going to smoke a cigar too?" I ask.

"If you have one."

"Smoked my last cigar on the balcony."

"Next time."

The bartender drops off our drinks.

Simon wraps his fingers around his short. Raises his glass. "Cheers."

I copy the gesture. "Cheers."

He watches as I bring the cocktail glass to my lips.

Mmm. Gin, lemon, floral liqueur. The perfect mix of sweet and tart.

"And you?" he says. "Ordering an Aviation?"

"I like purple."

His eyes flit to my wine lips. "I've never seen you in purple."

"You keep track?"

"A color-coded diary."

Is that a joke? I'm too surprised to laugh. "The color of my outfit?"

"What else?"

Another joke. What the fuck? I actually smile.

We've known each other for a long time. More than fifteen years now. We're not just old classmates.

Our families are friends.

Our companies—I run a nonprofit, he runs a cybersecurity corporation—attend the same events.

We see each other once or twice a month. We make polite conversation. We ignore our past rivalry and current sexual tension.

Occasionally, he teases me about trying to save the world.

And I tease him about having all the money in the world.

No jokes.

Never jokes.

Lingering stares, yes—I can't help it, he *wears* his designer suits—but never jokes.

"Do you really drink it because it's purple?" he asks.

"I drink it because I like it."

"You drank gin in high school," he says.

"You brought five-hundred-dollar bottles of whiskey to parties in high school."

"You noticed."

His eyes fix on me.

They're dark and intense, like the deepest parts of the ocean.

He watches as I take a sip. Watches my lipstick mark the glass. "What was it you called me then? The Prince of Darkness."

I did.

"Do you still see me that way?"

"By now, you're the king."

He smiles. "Is that a compliment or an insult?"

"An observation."

"You don't like me?"

"Do you care?"

"Yes."

It hangs in the air. He cares what I think of him. He's sitting here, intense and unreadable, and interested in my opinion of him.

"But you're right. I'm not here for polite conversation."

Right about what?

Wait.

He's not here to talk.

Then—

Fuck.

"I want to fuck you." His voice is matter-of-fact and sure, like he's complimenting my dress, not professing his desire to see me out of it.

"You want to fuck me?"

"Yes. I have a room upstairs. A suite. We can stay here, talk about the gala, or your sister's wedding, or my resemblance to Beelzebub. Or we can go upstairs." Intent drops into his voice.

He turns to me. Brings every bit of his attention to me.

My stomach flutters. My thighs shake.

My brain tries to cut in. To remind me, Simon Pierce is a spoiled rich boy turned stuck-up suit.

But I'm too lost in his blue eyes.

He's too handsome.

He's way too handsome.

"It's up to you, Vanessa," he says. "Do you want to stay? Or do you want to go?"

Get Ruthless Rival Now

Author's Note

Ruthless Rival was one of the hardest books I've written. Not because of the book really (though I do struggle with the whole "external plot" thing). Because of where I was in my life. My back issues were acting up. And the appointments, for various ways to treat these issues, were taking over my life. Which left little time to write. Or energy to attend to other hobbies. And the relationships in my personal life? Not good. I didn't have the energy to open up Scrivner. Or so I thought.

When I finished *Ruthless Rival*, I wanted to be done with this series that I associated with such an unpleasant time. I did not want to write *Tempting Teacher*. But every time I thought about the story, I felt a little better. And when I finally started putting words to paper?

I remembered who I was. I remembered what moved me. Exploring interesting characters, watching them come together, inviting others to follow their journey.

I'm a lot of things, but I'm always a writer first, with everything that means: the love of language, the passion for narrative, the thirst for knowledge, the desire to explore nuanced, interesting ideas, the need for truth.

I need to write things that feel real and honest. I need to write things that resonate in unexpected ways. That doesn't necessarily mean they're "realistic" from every point of view. But they need to feel honest, from an emotional and character point of view. I need to believe these are real people, acting in a real way. And the thing about people is--

They act in all sorts of strange, unusual ways. And it's always fascinating to watch.

I'm a writer, before I'm anything else. And I'm grateful I write full time, but it means other concerns push my desire for truth, for compelling, resonant ideas out of the driver's seat. Sometimes, a desire to sell, or a need to hit a trope, or a promise to finish a series take over. And, sometimes, I forget what matters to me.

Writing something honest and compelling and playful in the best possible way. Whether I write a lighthearted romcom or an angsty as hell romance, I always want to inject a certain playfulness in my books. Sometimes I laugh because I'm happy and sometimes I laugh so I don't cry, but I always need that sense of levity.

And that is real. People don't behave in stereotypical ways. They don't cry all night because of grief and feel only sadness. They feel all sorts of conflicting emotions: frustration, relief, anger, pride, joy, regret, satisfaction. And sadness.

My mom died when I was writing *Dirty Wedding*. And, ever since, grief has been on my mind. It touched everything I've written. It took over this series. Part of saying goodbye to the Pierces is letting go of this hold on grief. And that's scary, because, in a way, it's letting go of another connection to my mom.

But it's time.

My mom was a lot of things and our relationship was complicated. But she was always proud of me. And she was always impressed by my drive and creativity. I'm lucky I had that. Don't get me wrong. I had plenty of issues with both my parents (hi Dad!), but I never lacked support for my creative endeavors. I grew up believing my goals and ambitions were important. I grew up believing art was important, a way to explore ideas, express yourself, communicate with others, bring people together.

Not everyone has that.

With my books, I always hope to "spread the message." Not just the importance of art, creativity, self-expression (though that too--there's a reason I've written so many tattoo artists and rock stars). But the value of supporting women's ambitions and goals. Most of the time, I never say never, but I can confidently say I will never write a book that dismisses women's ambitions. I will never write a hero who sees his partners' goals as a threat.

(And before you say *Dangerous Kiss*, that's not *really* why Ethan and Violet broke up. But it's not my place to say how anyone should interpret the book).

As much as I'm (okay want to be) a total boss bitch bad ass, I'm a softie deep down. I love love and I want to see people fall in love and support each other as partners (in fun and surprising ways). That's what romance is. And that's what Max and Opal do.

Thanks for going on this journey for me.

I hope you enjoyed this book. But even more, I hope you felt deeply. I hope you found new insights on the world, people, relationships, yourself.

Love,
Crystal

Acknowledgments

My first thanks goes to my husband, for his support when I'm lost in bookland and for generally being the sun in my sky.

The second goes to my father, for insisting I go to the best film school in the country, everything else be damned. I wouldn't love movies, writing, or storytelling half as much if not for all our afternoon trips to the bookstore and weekends at the movies. You've always been supportive of my goals, and that means the world to me.

A big shout out to all my beta readers. And also to my ARC readers for helping spread the word to everyone else in the world.

To all my writer friends who talk me down from the ledge, hold my hand, and tell me when my ideas are terrible and when they're brilliant, thank you.

Thanks so much to my editor Marla, and to Hang Le for the cover design.

As always, my biggest thanks goes to my readers. Thank you for picking up *Tempting Teacher*.